RIVER MERMAID

christy goerzen

CRWTH PRESS

Library and Archives Canada Cataloguing in Publication

Title: River mermaid / Christy Goerzen.
Names: Goerzen, Christy, 1975- author.
Identifiers: Canadiana 20210263326 | ISBN 9781989724101 (softcover)
Classification: LCC PS8613.O38 R58 2021 | DDC jC813/.6—dc23

Cover design by Erin Green
Interior design by Teresa Bubela
Copy edited by Renée Layberry
Proofread by Audrey McClellan

Crwth Press gratefully acknowledges the support of the Province of
British Columbia through the British Columbia Arts Council.

Crwth Press
#204 - 2320 Woodland Drive
Vancouver, BC V5N 3P2
www.crwth.ca

MIX
Paper from
responsible sources
FSC
www.fsc.org   FSC® C103214

For Tara, with buckets of love
I'm so glad we share a brain.

Art Class

"Mercedes."
Ms. Keyes beckons me to her desk
with a flick of her paint-covered hand.
"I'm guessing since you haven't burst
into class with the good news,
you haven't heard yet."

"Not yet," I say.
"But don't worry, Ms. K. Other than
my parents, you'll be the first to know."

"Any day now," she says.

Any day now.
When you're waiting
for something important,
days become months.

Talent Crush

Photos of singers and actors decorate the other kids' lockers:
guitars over shoulders,
tattoos on arms,
pouts on flawless faces.

In my locker are photos of
seaweed and driftwood spirals,
one hundred snowballs cradled between two trees,
office chairs scattered like autumn leaves through a forest.

Environmental art
and large-scale sculpture
make fireworks explode
on the right side of my brain.

Nils-Udo, Andy Goldsworthy, Ted Friesen.
I don't care about their eyes
or their voices or their clothes —
it's their talent I'm crushing on.

"Oooh, Ted," my best friend Sandra's
voice booms into my ear.
(Not a quiet one, that Sandra.)
"So sexy. I love you." She sticks out her tongue
and gives the photo a salacious air-lick.

"Ew," I say, putting my hand over the photo of
Ted Friesen's 1994 Amsterdam sculpture.
"Don't mess with the sacredness of the Ted."

She slaps my butt as she heads
over to her own locker.
Exchanges like this are on the daily.

I turn back to my photos.

A black-and-white photo of
Nils-Udo's *The Nest* is at eye level
on my locker door.
Birch sticks laid in a perfect circle,
lines straight and true like a geometric formula.
I touch the middle of that nest
like a lucky rabbit's foot
before I close my locker door.

Just one more class,
before I can run home
and check the mail again.

Part-Time Mother

My mom is an artist,
and a mother,
but never both at once.

She's in her studio
soldering copper,
pounding rivets,
polishing iron.
Too engrossed in her work to
respond to my greeting
as I stop by her studio door.

When she's finished this piece
she'll buy milk and toilet paper,
ask me about school and
make homemade soup.
But not before then,
never before.

It's always been like this.

I knock again, louder.
She looks up, smiles her
wide easy smile.

"Hi, hon," she says, wiping a length
of rebar with a cloth.
"I didn't see anything in the mail
today, did you?"

I shake my head and lean against her door,
all dramatic.

"I remember waiting for my letter," she says.
"You never forget that ache
of anticipation, you know?"

Do I ever.

She sets down her rebar
and crosses her calloused fingers.

"We'll pop a bottle of Asti
when you get it," she says.

"Classy," I say, and head into the
kitchen to rummage around for a snack.

Contemporaries

Later,
I'm on my bedroom floor.

A black-and-white photo of
Andy Goldsworthy's *Melt* is in front of me,
dog-eared in my copy of *Sculptors of the Modern Era*.

I flip to *Desks* by Ted Friesen,
which stuns me every time.

More than 300 office desks
stacked end to end
to resemble an office tower.
"A social commentary on the rat race and
the oppression of the white collar,"
the description says.

These works of art are my visual playlist.

My mother has her own entry in
Sculptors of the Modern Era.

Her bright face, her wide easy mouth
smiling out from page 287.
Rough, silver ring-clad fingers brushing her cheek,
hair shaggy around her face,
looking every bit the badass artist.

Patrice Stowell, 1970 –

A Canadian artist and sculptor known for her use of recycled
metal and found materials, Stowell is best known for her
work *Presence* (2007), a large-scale piece that featured
more than two hundred life-size mannequins created with
found metal objects. A commentary on the anonymity of
modern life, *Presence* won the Leon Hansfield Diamond
Award, one of the pre-eminent sculpture prizes in the world.
Stowell's works have focused on social justice themes such
as feminism, women's rights and the peace movement.
Now one of the world's leading creators of public art pieces,
Stowell's work can be seen throughout Canada, the US,
Europe, Japan and Australia.

I've read this a hundred times, a thousand times.
Stabs of envy and flashes of pride —
that's my mom, I giggle as I show my friends.

Mercedes Stowell, 2003 –

A Canadian found-materials artist based in New York City, Stowell is known for her use of objects from children's material culture, recycled building materials and the natural world. Stowell has created many critically acclaimed works that explore nostalgia, relationships and ecology. Her first major gallery exhibit, *They Have Souls* (2025), featured sculptures and installations created solely from her childhood possessions. The exhibit included works Stowell made while in high school, including her famous piece *Quality Time* (2018), a life-size couch decorated entirely in My Little Ponies. Stowell's work has been exhibited in more than three hundred galleries across North America, the United Kingdom, and Europe. A graduate of the renowned Wildwood Fine Arts School, Stowell holds a BFA magna cum laude from Yale University and an MFA from Harvard University. She has won many awards all over the world.

I read once that you should write
your own obituary,
how you'd like people to remember you
how you spent your life
what gave you meaning.

Instead I wrote
my entry in a future edition of
Sculptors of the Modern Era.

The Next Day, After School

It's there. A white business-sized
envelope, my name handwritten on the front,
Wildwood Fine Arts School in the upper left corner.

I yank it from the mailbox and
hold it tight to my heart as I run inside.

I rip open the envelope, backpack and shoes still on,
standing in the entryway.

Dear Miss Stowell:

*Thank you for your application to the Wildwood Fine Arts
School. We have reviewed your portfolio and images of your
original piece,* Quality Time.

I hold the letter to my heart again.
It's beating so hard my eyes are throbbing.

I keep reading.

*While we enjoyed your piece, we are unable to offer you
acceptance for the Grade 11 program. We suggest you spend
some time reflecting on your artistic intentions and execution,
as those are growth areas for you.*

*We do encourage you to apply for the Grade 12 Specialty Focus
program next year.*

Thank you for your interest in our school. We wish you all the best in your future endeavours.

Sincerely,

Helen Chan
Principal, Wildwood Fine Arts School

On behalf of the Selection Committee

Earnings

I let my backpack fall off my shoulders
onto the carpet
while I stand there, swaying.
The letter flutters to the floor.

My parents hear the sob.

"Mercedes?" I hear my mom's voice.

I sob louder.

Like cuckoos in a clock,
my mom and dad each pop out of their
side-by-side doors
(his office, her studio).

"Mercedes?" my mom says, rushing to me.
"What is it?"

I point to the letter on the floor.
She picks it up.

One glance and she knows. She looks at my dad.
They look at me.

"Damn," my dad says, rubbing his neck.
"I'd told everyone your acceptance
was just a formality."

"Paul!" My mom swats the air next to him.

"Wow, thanks for your support, *Dad*."
My voice is strangled through the tears.

My mom says something to my dad in lowered
tones. He turns and marches back
into his office without another word.

Wordlessly, my mom puts her arm around
my shoulder and leads me into the kitchen.

Kitchen Island

We sit, steaming cups
of chai between us.
I can't believe my mom is taking a break.
I guess she can make time when her daughter receives
The Worst News Ever in Her Entire Life.

I can't speak.
Wildwood was supposed to be
my gateway to
my future as an artist,
to Yale and Harvard
and international exhibitions.

"I thought I was in," I say, finally.
"So did Dad, apparently."

"Oh don't worry about him,"
my mom says.

"Yeah, but all the people I'll ever need to
impress will think the daughter
of the great Patrice and Paul Stowell
is a giant failure."

My mom puts a hand on my shoulder.
"Sweetie, I know this is hard,
but you're only sixteen. You have a huge future
ahead of you. And you don't have to go to Wildwood
to succeed as an artist."

"*You* went there," I say, taking a
loud slurp of my chai.

"Yes, but lots of others didn't. Try again
for Grade 12 if you want to."

I sigh. "They hardly accept anyone new in Grade 12."

She says that failure
is part of the artistic process.
That Cézanne and Van Gogh and
Mozart and Warhol had failures.
And she had failures.
"You have to learn from them
and move on."

I'm aware of her words,
but they float past me.

"I felt like *Quality Time* was a good piece,"
I say. "But they're telling me to
reflect on my artistic intentions."

I hate it when teachers say *reflecting*.

"And my execution," I say. "Are they talking about
all the staples and glue?"

"That was quite a night," my mom says.

I let out a tiny laugh. "It sure was."
I pause. "But I guess it wasn't good enough."

I'm full of confusion and anger
and shame and sadness and disappointment.
My brain doesn't know what
to do with itself.
My hands shake. My heart
bores a hole through my chest.

"These things are so subjective," my mom says. "Sometimes
I don't know why some of my pieces aren't accepted
into exhibitions."

"That's it." I fling my arms up and
let them fall back into my lap.
"I'm over. Why bother?"

"You don't mean that,"
my mom says.
"I do," I say, jaw set.

"You might feel differently tomorrow."
"I won't," I say.
"Oh, Mercedes," she says.
"My stubborn little Taurus."

And with that, she picks up her mug of chai,
gives me a pat on the shoulder and
heads back into her studio to create
more amazing, world-renowned art.

Survey

After I half-drink my tepid chai,
I wander around my bedroom.

My art stares at me from all angles.

Last Place
A quilt sewn from my childhood T-shirts
edged with dirty shoelaces and
fourth- and fifth-place ribbons
from cross-country races.

Dorothy
A tribute to my late grandmother.
Pantyhose, Sunday hat, dried flowers
patent leather shoes (actually hers),
glued to a canvas
covered in pages torn from the Bible.
(Controversial! Mom loved that.)

Downtrodden
A photo series. I laid out ten arrows
made of crow feathers and sticks
at the bus stop.
The arrows pointed toward the river,
the forest, nature.
At first people politely
walked around the arrows.
Some even paused to look.
But as more rushed to the bus stop

the arrows were stepped on, scattered,
spread about.
My photo essay, in black and white
for artistic effect, showed the arrows' progression
from tidy beginnings to their tattered downfall.

Drop cloths, paints
and stacks of cardboard, fabric. All over my floor.
Wood, bike spokes, doll parts and tea cups.
My ever-growing pile of "art junk,"
as my mom likes to call it.

The trinkets and memories and glue
(much, much glue)
of a girl from the suburbs
with big dreams.

In five minutes
I've pushed and crammed and
packed away every scrap of it
in my closet, on top of old ice skates.

I stack everything carefully,
because you never know.

I wander out to the garage,
where *Quality Time* has been sitting,
wrapped in thick, clear plastic
because I didn't know what else to do with it.
I push back the plastic,
regard the piece, hands on hips.

Fresh disbelief courses through me.
I fold up next to it on the cold concrete floor,
rock back and forth in the fetal position.

Why?
Why?
Why?

I thought I had it in the bag.
Dunzo. Nailed it.
Whatever other triumphant-sounding
cliché I could think of.

I stand, and I decide not to resist the
overpowering urge to kick those ponies in the ass.
My bare foot feels no pain as it strikes the hard plastic.
Stardash and Honeybelle fly across the garage
and hit the metal door with a *tink*.

I step on a fallen pony, squish it
under the ball of my foot
with all the might of my 115 pounds.

It flattens, then seconds later
puffs back into place,
like nothing bad ever happened to it.

The Next Day

I have to face Ms. Keyes
in art class.

She must see it on
my face before I
even tell her.

"Oh, my little bunny,"
Ms. Keyes says,
enfolding me in her comfortable arms.

It guts me like a fresh stab all over again.

I let myself melt into her
like a baby. Shaking with sobs.
Deftly, Ms. Keyes uses one foot
to close the door to her tiny office as
students start to shuffle into the art room.

Click.

Then, Between Classes

Sandra does her usual
stopping-by-my-locker thing.
She goes to tickle my side,
but I flick her away.

"Whoa, dude," she says,
backing up.
"What up?"

I sigh and close my eyes.
Lean against the frame
of my locker.
Tell her the news. It comes out like
a low grumble, under my breath.

Sandra gasps. "You mean ...
you'll be here next year?"
Her black-lined eyes are shining.
"And we'll get to grad together?"

I can't believe what I'm hearing.

"What the hell," I say. "It's only been
my lifelong *dream*.
No big deal."

"Oh," she says. "Sorry."

Pauses,
like she doesn't know
what to do now.
"Want to come over and watch
Ferris Bueller's Day Off tonight?
Drown your sorrows?
I'll get Twizzlers."
My favourite.

"Probably not," I say.
I slam my locker shut.
"But thanks," I add.

Even in my torment,
I don't want to hurt her feelings.

Wednesday, Thursday, Friday

Sandra tries to drag me out to the mall
"or something else fun,"
tries to be the buoyant Ferris Bueller
to my sullen Cameron Frye.

I think this is me now.
Mope-a-rama.

Several Months Later

Art can be your job
my parents had said
when I was around
thirteen, or fourteen,
when the other kids were starting to
babysit or deliver papers or bag groceries.
I didn't want to get one of those jobs,
but it seemed like something that
maybe I should try.

My mother said,
"I'm happy to see you work on your art
instead of making caramel macchiatos and
mopping floors."

They stopped saying that three months ago.

Job Fair

I find a 7-Eleven application
under my bedroom door
one day. Then one for Starbucks,
and today, McDonald's.
McDonald's, of all places.

I march down to my mom's studio.
"What is *this*?" I say,
waving the papers in the air.

"Mercedes," my mom says.
"I would love to see
you work on some pieces, but ..."
She throws her hands in the air.

My father looks at me over his glasses
for a second before turning back
to his papers.
"We're not going to finance
your *Juxtapoz* subscription if all
you're doing is sulking in your room."
That hit me where it hurt. *Juxtapoz*.
My favourite art magazine.

I take the stack of crappy-job applications
and rip them up, right in front of them.
Then I stomp up to my room.
Very mature, I know.

And So

It takes some time,
but by the end of summer break
I decide I want to try
to be normal.

Screw the noise inside my head
the midnight cringes
the stew of disappointment
still strong after all these months.

Instead of scoffing at
the shallowness of everyone at school
and distancing myself,
I'm going to embrace it.
It will be easier, I think.

At the mall with Sandra
after Grade 11 starts
we get samples at Nespresso,
eyeliner and lipstick at Sephora
and browse the T-shirts at Hot Topic.

In the food court, over bubble teas with extra pearls
and New York Fries, she tells me about kissing cute boys
behind the bleachers in the gym.
And I talk about my crush on the boy in math class.

We giggle.
The pearls from the bubble tea go *blip blip blip*
up the straw, down my throat,
like little bursts of delight.

This is easy,
I think.

I like this.

BFF

Sandra and I met in kindergarten.
Her: gap-toothed and wearing a
flowery dress that she hated.
Me: forever in a daydream,
my limp hair in braids and
plastic barrettes.
During story time on the carpet,
with sure fingers, she would loosen the braids
and fluff up my hair.
I looked forward to story time every day.

We took ballet together. We both sucked.
We giggled in Girl Guides.
She helped me with math;
I helped her with English.
She talked to me about the boys she was
in love with, and I listened.
Sleepovers, movie nights,
all of it — she's like a sister to me.

I was always the kid who
carried around my sketchbook,
made abstract sculptures out of pipe cleaners
and spoke, impassioned, about
artistic fame and success.

Sandra would always say something like,
"Oh, you and your art."

Then she'd change the subject,
to boys or movies or
whatever.

It's always been a bit of a thing.

Rites of Passage

In the food court,
still sipping bubble tea,
I tell Sandra my parents
want me to get a "regular" job.

"You know, dude," she says, "I'm not saying
I'm on your parents' side, but don't knock
it until you've tried it."

Sandra has been working
at her parents' café, Hit the Spot,
since she was thirteen.

"If you want a 'regular job'" — her sparkly
blue nails make air quotes — "I could get
you some shifts. It's mostly serving
the old ladies their little pots of tea
and carrot cake."

I sip in silence, thinking.
Sandra could be right.
It might be fun.

"It could be like a TV show," I say.
"They always work in fun coffee shops
in sitcoms."

Sandra side-eyes me.
"What are you trying to tell me, Stowell?"

"You know what I'm saying, Polinsky."

Sandra's usual dry expression is suddenly
filled with more glee than I've ever seen
in all our years of best frienddom.

"Really?"

I nod.

"We'll make up our own theme song.
We can make all the free
hazelnut lattes we want,"
I say, not skipping a beat.

"Play our own music instead of
that crap my parents play."

"Heck yes," we say at the same time.

Laughing,
we high-five.

Hit the Spot

Two days later it's
done and dusted.
The job, I mean.
I'll be wiping tables and
serving apple strudel
with Sandra,
two or three shifts per week.

She shows me the espresso maker
the hand-wash station
my apron and name tag.
And it's like she still can't
believe I'm here.
Neither can I,
to be honest.

"Let's play Odin's Sire.
See if anyone notices."
Odin's Sire is her new boyfriend's band.
They play "melodic death metal."

A couple of old dudes
in the corner are
talking about their
arthritis medication.

A woman in a pink track suit
is idly rocking a baby in a stroller back and forth
while flipping through *People* magazine.

The opening chords buzz.
Not too loud, but loud enough.
The mother looks around,
goes back to the Kardashians.
One of the old dudes covers his
left ear and keeps talking.

Sandra crouches behind the counter,
bent over in a laugh.
I can see she already has it
completely planned out:

All the Fun We're Going to Have.

Fumbling Toward Normalcy

I mess up peoples' change.
I heat up one old lady's croissant too much.
I make a guy's Americano too weak,
but not too bad for a first day.

After closing,
Sandra pumps Lizzo.

We sing about feeling good as hell
as we mop, then
make ourselves fancy coffees with
flavoured syrups.

I could get used to this.

Sum Total

The next day, I have math after lunch.

And I'm thinking about
Everything I Know About Him:

- Name: Ellis McShay (deliciously literary/Scottish)
- Moved here from Ontario at the beginning of the school year
- His only friend appears to be Jeb (ugh)
- He's part Japanese
- Has a T-shirt that reads *Oh the humanity*

And most tantalizingly:
on his binder he's written
the straight line is a godless line
a quote from Austrian artist and
architectural designer Hundertwasser.

I didn't even have to look that up.
But anyway,
he has an art quote on his binder.
We're so meant to be together.

That quote could be the perfect entry point.
"Oh, Hundertwasser," I could say.
"Love his Green Citadel."
But could I ever pluck up the courage to say that?

Doubtful.

Palettes

Art class: colour theory day.
Ms. Keyes circles the room
like she always does,
ruminates and runs her fingers
through her short wild hair, over and over.

"Blues and greens are the cool colours,
representing safety and calm and trust."
Like the river.
And trout tails.

"Reds and oranges and browns are the warm colours —
passion and autumn leaves."
Like stop signs.
And dumpster fires.

I spin the colour wheel
around and around,
mesmerized by the streaks of
orange and red and green and blue
warm cool warm cool warm cool,
while I'm supposed to be
identifying triadic combinations.

I feel a slight rustle at my elbow.
There, jotted on a pale blue paint swatch:
Let's chat after class.

She's stealthy,
that Ms. Keyes.

I tried to switch,
not take art this year,
and was in Home Ec with Sandra
(much to her temporary delight).

But in the end
Ms. Keyes convinced me.
"If nothing else," she'd said,
"at least take this."
(*This* meaning Art 11.)
"Please."

And because I adore Ms. Keyes —
her combination of tough love and
quirk and drama —
I finally said yes.

But I'm not going to lie:
I regret my decision most days.
Sitting here, surrounded by
paints, canvases, wire and clay,

none of this inspires me now.

3:01 p.m.

"Mercedes,"
Ms. Keyes says
in that musical way of hers.
"How are you?"

She scratches her forehead, swiping
four perfect lines of hot pink paint
onto her dark skin.
The bright pink against the smooth brown
is so stunning I want to take a photo of it.

"I'm fine," I say with a small smile.

"So here's the thing,"
she says.
"You're failing this class."

She's not one to soften a blow,
that's for sure.

"You haven't done the still life,
the mixed media or the clay model."

"I told you I didn't want to be here," I say.
I start to stand up, but
she blocks my path with her arm.

"I want to help you pass,"
she says. "You don't flunk
Paul and Patrice Stowell's daughter
from art class, all right?"

I stare at her a moment,
unblinking.
"Oh fine, if that's what it's about,"
I say.

"Come on, I'm kidding," she says.
(But I'm sure that this is, in fact,
part of the reason.)

"I want you to do a self-directed assignment.
Something you love. Something you're inspired by.
Forget these other assignments,"
she says, throwing a sheaf of paper
into the air, high into the art room ceiling.
The papers float down over us
like a snowfall of high school bureaucracy.
I laugh. She laughs.

"Okay," I say, dubious. "Thank you."
Because I'm grateful, I really am.

Even if making art right now
is about as exciting to me as
putting together IKEA furniture.

"Mercedes, I know it's still in there,"
she says, her deep brown eyes
staring straight into mine,
like she's trying to will
sparks to fly.

I turn to go.

"And if you're happy with it,"
she says, "I want you to use it to apply
to Wildwood. Consider this my
not-so-gentle nudge."

I look back at her hopeful face.

"There's still a chance."

"No, there isn't,"
I say.

Attempts

Friday after school
I'm on my bedroom floor.
In our meeting, Ms. Keyes
said she wants to see
"a beginning sketch of an idea"
from me by Monday.
Three days.
I haven't taken any action
yet.

But the thought of failing,
the thought of an F
in *art*, no less
(that would besmirch
the Stowell family name,
I'm sure) —
it just can't happen.

Three hours later,
it's like an ugly-art-projects
bomb exploded in here.
Stuff is strewn everywhere.

I've dragged out the supplies
I carefully stacked in my closet
months ago.

I numbly paw through it all. It feels foreign,
surreal,
looking at everything again.

I've ripped apart old bedsheets
covered in smiling, suit-wearing rabbits,
to make some sort of sculptural skirt.
I pin, I drape, I twirl the fabric into
roses of faded flannel.

Nope, never mind.
It looks like a four-year-old's
sewing project.

I find a box of old makeup
in the downstairs bathroom,
crumbling and stinky.
I lay the Avon lipsticks and
Maybelline mascara tubes crosswise,
like a pink and green log cabin,
with a brush tree out front.
Cute, but stupid.

On my bookshelf, my phone
buzzes with a text.

Laity's

Party at Laity's barn tonight.
Carl's working. Come with me.

Sandra's text shocks me out of my torment.

I'm coming over to make you look cute.
Do you have any good booty jeans?

Sandra always messages me in proper English.
She knows I hate text shorthand,
not to mention emojis.
I'm sure her texts to other friends are
full of smiley faces and
jumbles of letters barely resembling words.
She's a good friend to me that way.

I'm busy.
I text back.
I'm failing art.
I should work on stuff.

Next thing I know, my phone's ringing.
(Ring tone: "Popcorn," set by Sandra, of course,
because she knows it bugs me.)

"Mercedes. It'll be fine.
You'll be fine.
I'm coming over."

I drop my phone on my bed.
There's no use trying to resist
the power of the Sandra.

My stomach grumbles.
I head to the kitchen,
rustle through bags of
stale chips, Styrofoam boxes
of rotting Chinese takeout.
Not even a can of soup to heat up.

Bring me a cranberry scone?
I text Sandra.

Sorry, already left the café.

Damn.

Eight o'clock already.
It's peanut butter and jam sandwiches for me.
Except the Smucker's jar is empty,
only a dried scab of strawberry stuck to the lid.
With no jam to temper it,
peanut butter lodges itself
on the roof of my mouth,
Silly Putty on the ridge behind my front teeth.

I wonder if they've eaten.
My mother usually survives on
black coffee and crackers at this point,
and my father, forever at her side,

will roll a piece of black licorice
around in his mouth for hours
like chewing tobacco.

It's like this in the Stowell house
when she's at the end, the final countdown,
when my mother has "just six more rivets to go."
Just a minute just a minute just a minute.

I take out the peanut butter jar again
slap four pieces of bread on the counter
(give my dad the heels),
scrape the jar with a butter knife —
just enough for two sandwiches.
Cut my mom's diagonal, as she likes
and leave my dad's whole,
because whatever.
Put a couple of grapes on the side
for a sad little garnish.

"I'm going to Laity's with Sandra," I say,
plopping the plates in front of them
as they work, side by side, in my mother's studio.
"Be back late."

"Okay," my mom says, "have fun."
"We're almost done here," my father says,
not looking up, as usual.

Sandra, Continued

Sandra bustles in ten minutes later,
her hair swept over,
freshly shaved on the right side of her head,
a touch of shimmery green eyeshadow
and clear lip gloss.

She's tall and broad-shouldered and
quite regular looking,
but she's learned how to work it.
Hand perpetually on one curvy hip, chin tipped up
slightly, good posture.
She's got the confidence.

"So," she says, eyebrows wiggling up and down,
"rumour has it that *Ellis* might be there tonight."

I groan.
I don't know if that makes me want to go
more, or less.

"It'll do you good to get out," she says.
"Stop worrying about school for a bit."

Because, of course, it would never occur
to Sandra to concern herself with school.

"He'll never like me," I say.
"We need to get you some action," she says.
"Loosen you up a little.
You remind me of my grandma half the time."

I sigh. She's said that before.

"Now, hold still. Sandra's about
to work her magic."
She props me up in front of the
little mirror on my dresser,
digs through a bag of makeup
she brought from home.

"Your eyes remind me of laser beams," Sandra says,
fussing over me with a brown eyeliner pencil.
"Definitely your best feature."

She's not the first person to tell me this.
Also aunts, grandfathers, my mom
and other relatives ... no one of real consequence.

As though my eyes need to work extra hard
to compensate for my
lank brown hair and narrow shoulders,
pointy chin and big eyebrows.

Sandra rummages through
her brushes and eyeshadows and lipsticks,
clicking and clacking together quietly,
applying them to my face with
intent.
Calm washes over me,
makes my eyelids droop.

A brush of bronzer, light peachy eyeshadow,
lip gloss.
Done.

"Okay, where's that black tank top —
the one you wore to Kaylee's birthday dinner
last month. It makes your boobs look bigger."

She pushes me and prods me
into the tank top, until I have
something resembling cleavage.
My dark jeans and
black ankle boots with the fringe,
also selected by Sandra,
complete the look.

It's strange, seeing myself like this.
Most of the time I don't think
about my body at all.
It's just the thing that carries my head around.

"Girls," my mom calls to us from the kitchen.
Sandra and I go downstairs.
Mom holds up a bottle of red wine,
its golden label gleaming.
"A glass before you go?"

"No thanks," I say.
"Yes please!" Sandra chimes in at the same time.
I elbow her, but she heads
in my mother's direction anyway. I sigh and follow.

"Sandra, how are you, darling?" my mom says,
passing a goblet of pinot noir.
"We're driving," I say. "We shouldn't have any."

"We'll share," my mom says, winking at Sandra.
Quickly, my mom pops a red pill into her mouth
and takes a swig. I can see it's a Tylenol.

"Headache," my mom shrugs,
before I can even ask.

The pleasure at the invitation
is evident in Sandra's little smile.
But she plays it cool, sitting on one side
of the kitchen island, my mom on the other,
the goblet of wine in the middle.
And me, hovering, restless.

Sandra's telling my mom about
her boyfriend and her geology exam, asking
about my mom's latest commissions,
laughing in between.

"Shouldn't we be going?" I say.
I always get nervous before social events,
worried I'll say the wrong thing or look awkward,
and just standing here is killing me.

"Jeez, Stowell, it would do you good to take a sip,"
Sandra says, holding the goblet up to my mouth.
I smell the acrid vinegar of the wine
and screw up my face.

My mom laughs. Sandra laughs.
They have an easy way together.
It annoys me.

"Your mom is the best,"
Sandra says a few minutes later
as the front door slaps closed behind us,
and we head toward her old black Civic.

"I'll drive," I say, and Sandra doesn't balk.

"I wish my mom was more like
your mom," she says, buckling up
on the passenger side.

She says this whenever I complain
about not having any clean socks
or a hot meal other than Mr. Noodles
in a week.

Sandra sees only the long hair,
orange and gold and white like a campfire,
the tall leather boots
rings on each finger and raspy laugh,
limbs lithe like a modern dancer.

It's true, though —
when my mom is good,
she's really, really good.

Sandra's mom doesn't announce
spontaneous dance parties under the full moon.
Sandra's mom doesn't speak Swedish, Swahili and Russian
thanks to foreign artist-in-residence stints.

"Your mom is the best,"
Sandra says, nodding her head.
Hair, blond with blue tips,
swinging to one side.

The Queen of Unrequited Love

Love and other sharp pointy things,
Sandra signs every email,
every DM.
Often LAOSPT for short.

I never really understood this until
Ellis McShay came along.

Just the thought of him gives me that
stiletto-heel kick in my chest,
every time.

"So, what'll you do when you see Ellis?"
Sandra asks, drawing out the syllables in his name playfully.
Her voice jolts me back to reality
as we bump along the road to Laity's.

Her car's old struts slam and clack with each pothole,
a six pack of beer in her trunk.
I bought it, of course, because I never get ID'd.

I'll fake-drink them; I always do —
touch the bottle to my lips
and then pour it out when no one's looking.
Pretend to have a buzz.
I get drunk off their drunk anyway.

"He probably won't even be there," I say, looking over.
I see the shimmer of glitter on Sandra's eyelids
in the headlights from oncoming cars.

He's never there. Overprotective father, apparently.
It's not like I'd talk to him anyway.
I wish I could be easy with guys like Sandra is,
bumming a cigarette even though she doesn't smoke,
or sharing her bottle of beer,
standing with her lower back arched prettily.

I don't even know how to
interact normally with people,
let alone make jokes
or flirt.
Sometimes I think I might be an alien.

"Jesus," Sandra says, as I make a sharp turn.
"I can hear your heart beating from here.
Just chill."

But I can't do that.
I just can't.

Laity's, Part Two

The second we arrive,
I regret my fashion choices.
A tank top in January
is a stupid idea.
Sandra grabs a black pashmina from
the back of the car,
tells me to wear it off my shoulders
if I can.

Our flimsy boots squelch
in the half-frozen mud,
the flames calling to us from
beyond the fence posts.

There have been a dozen parties
here already this year,
maybe more,
but this is only the second time
I've let Sandra drag me
to the barn that Michelle Laity's dad
has made the unofficial party house
for generations of Maple Ridge kids.

Barrel fires circle the barn doors.
Kids slouch around them in the cold,
hoodies up, hot chocolate in their Bailey's.
Between the fires and the stars,
I can barely see their faces.

The air smells of weed,
cheap beer and winter.
A couple of guys playing djembes
next to the fence
nod and smile.

Bottles are clinked
and soon after tossed into the mud.
"Let's go inside,"
Sandra says. "See if there's
anyone here of significance."

Over There

"He's here!" Sandra exclaims
too loudly,
after we find a sawhorse
to sit on inside the barn.
We share it with a girl
named Rain, who we've just met.

I casually fake-sip my Bud Light.
I don't want to look, but I do.
Beyond the brown bottle raised to my lips
I see him,
across the barn, sitting with Jeb
next to a dried-out Christmas tree,
tinsel still clinging to its brownish branches.

I get that jolt in my heart
whenever I look at him —
especially now
as our eyes meet.

It's the first time we've made eye contact.
Although I've been staring
at him for the past four and a half months.

Him:
rolled-up jeans
white T-shirt
black bangs
swooping over next to his left eye.

Out of my league.

He sits with his legs crossed at the ankles,
dark eyes narrowed
looking straight at me.
I think he's the one with the laser beams.

I look away first.

Forget the jolt in my heart;
there's a bony stab in my right side.
"He just looked *right* at you!"
Sandra shout-whispers.

I elbow her back
harder,
and breathe, "Shut up."

Calmly,
Sandra grasps my left wrist
pulls me outside
past a group of girls belting Disney songs,
around to the side of the barn.

"Mercedes, you *have* to go talk to him!"
she says, ever the bossy best friend.
I shake my head so ferociously
I see stars.
"Come *on*," she growls,
"this is your chance."

"It could mean anything that
he looked at me. It doesn't mean
I should talk to him."

"Yes it does."

"No," I say,
"I'm not like you. I can't
talk to guys.
What would I say?"

"Offer a beer. Ask to sit.
Anything."

I shake my head again. I can smell
the Finesse mousse that
Sandra liberally applied.
"Nope. Can't.
Besides, Jeb's a dick."

"Whatever."
Sandra shrugs, then joins some guys
from the basketball team
around a barrel.

Sandra does this. Mini temper tantrums
over my lack of action.
My breath huffs in and out,
white puffs of steam
in the winter air.

When I go to stand beside her
ten minutes later
she wraps her arm around me
and leaves it there.

Always forgiven.

His 'n' Hers

11:30 p.m. now,
back from Laity's.
Nothing happened, of course —
I hung out with Sandra, and he left early.

My parents are both still working away,
Mom in her studio, Dad in his office.
From the couch, flipping through
a book of surrealist art,
I can see both doors,
one open, one closed.

I imagine my dad in his office
arranging my mother's calendar,
adding up receipts, predicting annual earnings.
Just then, his door swings open and he barges
through the open studio door, phone and papers in hand.
He doesn't see me.

"Looking good," he says, probably barely
glancing at her work-in-progress, like usual.
"I signed for that Berlin commission."

"But I already have the Moscow and Seoul pieces.
Those are huge."

"You can do it," my dad says, gruff.

"It's too much sometimes, Paul."

Silence.

"I've been having these headaches," my mom says.
"I was hoping for a break after this one."
(Massive tree sculpture she's been working on.)

Short pause.

"In all the years I've known you, hon,
you've never needed a break."

Chuckling, shaking his head,
my dad strides back into his office.
He still doesn't see me.

He almost never sees me.

Night Mom

Tomorrow it'll be salmon and mango fajitas,
or cauliflower and Stilton soup with crusty bread,
glasses of wine,
red red red like my mother's MAC lipstick,
donned to celebrate the completion
of another project.

The last rivet will have been riveted,
the metal polished.
The entire gigantic arbutus tree,
branches raised like strong copper arms,
will be meticulously wrapped
and shipped off,
where it will grace a street corner in Kitsilano —
for forever, I guess.

Another public artwork to line the streets,
another piece of recycled metal
with rivets from old pipes.

She is everywhere I go, everywhere I look.
You can't escape my mother.
Her tuba sculpture outside the Starbucks downtown.
Her dolphin made from heating ducts at the library.
Her curved archway of old paint cans
outside Waterfront Station.

These pieces sing at me in my peripheral vision
whenever I'm near them, my sketchbook in front of me,

trying to command my own
burst of genius.
She makes it look so easy.

And I can't even get a silly
high school art class assignment
right.

I decide to go check on her.

Outside her doorway I hear
the crunch of metal grinding into metal.

"Night, Mom," I say, looking in.
Seconds pass,
maybe minutes.
"Night, sweetie," she says at last.
She sets down her drill and smiles.

Rattling a near-empty bottle of Tylenol next to her,
she tips three tiny red pills into her hand and
swallows them without water.

"You okay?" I ask.
Her temples are red from so much
circular rubbing.

"I'm fine.
Come sit with me,"
she says,
"while I finish."

These invitations are rare.
I pull up a stool, watch as she
etches her initials onto a small copper plate.

She's so steady, so sure.
It's mesmerizing.

Suddenly, she drops her Dremel tool.
Her hands slam the table top,

hard.

Her eyes are closed,
head lolling to one side
jerking back
in a terrifying way.

It goes on for a minute,
maybe more.
It feels like twenty.

I stand up, frozen,
open my mouth to call for my dad,
but she snaps her head,
grabs my wrist
with her talon fingers,
says,

"No, no,
it's okay, Mercedes,
I'm just tired.

Tomorrow will be different.
Tomorrow will be better.
Tomorrow I'll be done."

She picks up her tool,
goes back to the etching.
Her hand shakes.
It never shakes.

I go to the kitchen,
my vision blurring with worry.
Make her a cup of tea
because I don't know what else to do.

Pieces of Tomorrow

I look for my mom and find her
in the kitchen,
reducing balsamic vinegar,
slicing free-range organic duck breasts,
stuffing them with blood orange and endive
as she dances around to Nirvana.

"Mom," I say,
"are you sure you're okay?
Last night was pretty freaky."
It haunted my dreams,
I add, in my head.

My mom waves her hand in the air,
dismissive.
"I'm just tired.
My naturopath says I have a
sensitive nervous system."

Kurt Cobain shriek-sings
here we are now, entertain us
and my mom shriek-sings along.

"I hated that goddamned arbutus tree,"
she says, turning the volume down.
She laughs,
and it sounds like rusty jingle bells.

Mom swings over a stool,
pours a glass of wine,
hands me a wooden spoon microphone
so I can sing too.

"But sometimes you have to make eight-foot-tall
arbutus trees to pay the mortgage,"
she adds.

"I don't ever want to have to compromise," I say.

"Sometimes you have to do work
for the money. It's business."

"Is that *Dad* talking? Capitalist," I say,
muffled in a jokey cough.

"Ooh, teenage attitude," my mom tsk-tsks,
then smiles. "No, that's
a balanced grown-up talking."

She sings again,
harmonizing with Kurt as he repeats
a denial, a denial, a denial, a denial.

My father keeps his phone on the table
during dinner.
Approximately every two point five minutes
it buzzes and
then his wide fingers clunk out a reply,
as he chews his food, mouth open.

"Honestly, Paul," my mom says,
"it can wait. This is our first family dinner
in two months."

"Sorry, hon," my dad says,
squinting as he pokes out the last few letters,
then drops the phone on the counter
behind him.

He gobbles down his duck and
boiled potatoes,
balls his napkin on his plate,
pats his belly,
heads to his office.

The Family Rock

After wine (which I drink, for once),
after a dance party
to Green Day (Mom's choice)
and Grimes (my choice),

Mom and I head down to
the family rock
by the river on the edge of our property
where she meditates every morning.

She raises her arms and breathes the
fresh cool air.
"I needed some of this," she says.
Giggling, she wades in only to her knees,
but still, it's crazy for January.

Her long green skirt
wraps around her
like a tail
like the tail of the river mermaid
from the story she's been telling me
since I was little.

I wade in,
gasping at the bracing chill,
but giggling too, my jeans heavy.

Because who wouldn't want
to follow a river mermaid.

Percolation

My mom has the rock,
and I have the roof.

There's a perfect little gable
outside my bedroom window,
slippery in the midnight dew.
I straddle the sandpaper shingles
that will line the sides of my calves
with hundreds of tiny scratches.

Late, late, late
and with a bright moon is best,
like tonight.

Then, ten minutes later:
About to watch
Say Anything.
Come over.
LAOSPT, S.

Currently on roof.
Contemplating life.

COME OVER.

Mr. Nice Bum

Sandra's already twenty minutes into the movie
but she rewinds it for me,
slips a Coke Zero into my hand,
throws me a pillow to sit on.

"I thought you had to spend the evening
flailing around in despair,"
she says, raising a pierced eyebrow.

"I decided to stop doing that, remember?"
I say. "Plus, how could I resist Mr. Nice Bum?"

We've watched it probably twenty times,
and we still swoon when
Lloyd Dobler holds up the boom box outside
Diane Court's window
his eyes shadowy and deep,
burning for her love.

Later, during one of the boring dad scenes,
Sandra says, "You know,
Ellis kinda looks like Mr. Nice Bum."
Her head jerks toward the TV.

When she says it I shiver.
It's like his actual name is
too sacred to be spoken aloud
at a normal volume.

And it's true, he does, more than a little.
Tall-ish,
dark hair
pale skin.

"Every girl wants her own Lloyd Dobler," she says.

The thought of it destroys me a little more.

During the next boring dad scene,
I'm gripped with the need to tell Sandra
about the day before.

I've been thinking about it all day,
sometimes in the back of my mind,
sometimes in the front.

"Seriously?" Sandra says, raising herself up on her elbows.
She pauses the movie.
"So it was a seizure?"

"I don't know," I say,
"but it was super scary."

"No kidding," Sandra says. "Jesus."

"Maybe she was so tired
that it was like falling asleep at the wheel
for a minute," I say.

"Did you tell your dad?"

I shake my head. "I overheard them talking.
My dad signed her up
for a bunch of new commissions. She told him
she needs a break. He just laughed."

I pause.

"He only cares about the money. Not the art."

"Your mom is a badass," Sandra says.
"She should just tell him
no more commissions right now."

I sigh. If only it worked that way.

Opening

The next night
my dad's wearing his leather jacket
and Old Spice.

That can only mean
they're either going to the pub
(The Frog & Nightgown, always)
or to an opening.

At the kitchen table I
try to act casual as I arrange a
bowl of pinecones into a turret.
The needles fit together nicely, like Lego.

Mom puts on her high-heeled boots,
Dad his polished black loafers,
without speaking.

"See you guys later?"
I pipe up
as Dad opens the front door.

"Just going to the art gallery,"
Mom says.
"Don't stay up too late.
School night."
The door clacks shut behind them.

Out of a perverse desire to further damage
my bruised spirit
I Google *Vancouver Central Gallery January 25.*

The Ben Jackson opening reception.

One of my favourite found-materials artists,
and they know it.

Twenty-three years old, from New York City.
Two years ago he
knit a ball gown entirely from
Barbie hair,
and the art world went wild.

Now *that* is what I'm talking about.

My parents used to take me to all
the openings, the galas, the receptions,
where I'd balance a tiny plate of
cheese and artisanal crackers
while my mom introduced me to
critics, bloggers, dealers, artists,
curators and gallery owners.
And my dad worked the room.

I turn over my iPad, push it away,
press more pinecones onto my turret,
walls, walls and more walls
until it becomes a castle.

I'm pissed at them, of course.
I feel it prickling up my spine,
making my ears burn.

I don't know
if they don't want me to go with them
or if they think I don't want to go.
These are things we don't talk about.

The castle walls finished,
I add a line of pinecones for a moat
to keep everyone out.

I dim the kitchen light
and gaze at my castle for a while,
seeing but not seeing.

Before I know it,
I raise my right arm and
knock the pinecone castle
off the table with one swipe.
It whacks the wall, clatters onto the floor,
breaks into dozens of little pinecones.

I turn and stomp up the spiral staircase,
round and round
to my room.

When I come down in the morning,
the pinecones are all back in the bowl.

Listening

My mom is waiting for me
in the living room,
a tray of coffee and
store-bought muffins on the
coffee table.

"I didn't have time to bake any,"
she says, gesturing at the plastic box.

"That's okay," I say,
taking one. "Thanks."

I'm suspicious about
her motives.

I want to bolt to my room
because I'm still
pissed off about the night before.
And I don't want to talk about
the pinecones or my art
or anything related.

But
when I get these moments with her,
these tiny openings in the clouds,
I want to drink her in like she's the rain and
I'm a plant in a summer drought.

"How's school going?"
she asks me
for the first time in months.

At first I just splutter
about biology and English
and history.
I don't mention art class.

Her hazel eyes are gazing right at me,
the golden flecks vibrant
in the morning sunlight.
Little red capillaries twist through the whites.

I feel my own pupils dilate
because, incredibly,
she's finally present.

This somehow compels me
to tell her I'm quite possibly,
rather imminently,
failing art class.

"Have you felt the pull to create?"
Mom says.

"No," I say. "But I don't care now.
I'm a regular person with
a regular job and a regular life.
And I'm fine with that.
It's easier."

My mom regards me for a moment,
looking flummoxed,
like she can't imagine what that
might feel like.

"I've been through creative blocks too, Mercedes.
But you've dreamed of being an artist
since, well, birth. Don't let one setback
have that much power over you."

"Easy for you to say."

"I'm worried about you," she says, then closes her eyes
and rubs her forehead. "I want you to be happy."

I sit up straight, square my shoulders. "I am.
But Mom, I'm worried about *you*. That, that
thing that happened to you ... that wasn't normal."

"We're talking about you right now, Mercedes, not me.
But anyway, it was just stress."

"You need to go to the doctor," I say.

"I'm fine," she says.

"Dad makes you work too hard."

"We make decisions together," she says.

"No you don't. I heard about the new commissions
you don't want to do."

"Oh, that," she says with a dismissive shrug. "It was a misunderstanding."

"Mom, the headaches. The seizure. You *need* to go to the doctor."

"Thanks for your concern, Mercedes, but I'm fine."

Full

I still have nothing
to show Ms. Keyes.
But I'm feeling better
and in about half an hour
I dash off
a pencil drawing of
my hand, holding the earth.
Straightforward, yes.
Inspired, no.

But it's better than the other
crap I attempted this weekend.

Waning

Mom shuffles into the kitchen,
robe on, hair in ponytail.

"You didn't go to the rock?"
I say.
This is strange;
she never misses a day.

I worry all over again
about whatever that was
when her head lolled and her limbs flailed,
and it was all very freaky.

She doesn't respond.
Her bare feet scuff over the
linoleum, to the sink.
She shakes the bottle of Tylenol.

Empty.

Square Inches

In math class we learn how to
calculate square measurements
and I don't even understand because
I'm more interested in the tendons in his forearms
rippling as he does the pen-twirling-around-his-thumb thing
over and over and over again.

This lucky 45-degree angle I have —
his desk, my desk —
allows me to gaze for an entire hour
at every last detail of his being
without him ever noticing.

Today's report:
Perfect bang swoop,
that dark beauty spot on
his upper right cheek,
grey V-neck T-shirt,
small hole on bottom hem,
a vein that runs deliciously
down the front of his bicep while
he does the pencil trick, and
the edge of a tattoo, possibly,
on the side of said bicep;
all I can see is a light green point.

Black jeans
and large feet in cool-looking purple shoes —
Tsubo, they read, beneath the laces.

I groan inside my head.

At the end of class,
pencil case in backpack,
backpack on shoulder,
I stand.

He brushes past me on his way out.
His elbow, my right breast.

He mumbles, "Sorry,"

and my ovaries explode.

Perfect English

Mr. Reed describes our
Grade 12 options to us:
English, English Literature,
Comparative Lit or
Creative Writing.

Passes out small green
pieces of paper,
asks us to indicate our
top two.

Sandra nudges me.
CW together? Easy A, amirite?
she's scrawled in
her notebook.

I nod,
smile tiny,
look out the window.

Because this isn't
how it was supposed to be.

Final Period

"So," Ms. Keyes says,
rubbing her hands together.
This week's hair colour:
teal blue with hints of yellow.
"What do you have for me?"

I take out the drawing,
smooth it onto the desk in front of her.

She picks it up.
I bite my nails, waiting.

"Technically, it's brilliant,"
she says.
"Nice shading, good light,
and you even drew all
the continents right."

She sets it down, fixes
her gaze on me.

"But what does it *mean*?"
she says.

Dammit. I knew she was going to ask me that.

"She's got the whole world
in her hand?"
I sing, half-hearted.

Ms. Keyes shakes her head at me.
"This is not you," she says.
"Try again."

I leave the art room,
wishing that sometimes
Ms. Keyes wouldn't be
quite so much of a hard-ass.

Sandra's waiting for me at my locker.
She starts jumping up and down
as soon as she sees me.

"What?" I say, still grouchy from art class.

"You're going to love this,"
she says, then pauses.

"Love what?"

"What's wrong with you, dude?" she says,
sensing my grump.

"You know how I'm failing art," I say.
"Ms. Keyes wants me to do some
extra assignments, and it's all garbage."

"I've got something that will cheer you up,"
she sings. "Apparently Ellis's family owns
a karate dojo in town. That new place, where
the camping store used to be."

"What does that matter?"

"Ellis teaches there."

That's all I needed to snap me out of it.

"Are you thinking what I'm thinking?"
I say, grabbing Sandra's hands.

"Drive by!"
we say together, jumping up and down.

Taigaa Karate

We go after school.
Sandra parks kitty-corner to the dojo,
where we can look in the windows
and not be noticed.

"Can you see anything?" Sandra says.

A bunch of kids mill around inside,
fluorescent lights bright
on their little karate outfits.
"Not really," I say.

"We'll wait," Sandra says, turning off the engine.

"He might not even be here tonight."

A few minutes later, the kids
assemble themselves in rows.
They're tiny, maybe four or five years old.
Two guys stand at the front.
I squint, and I can see just well enough.
One of the guys is Ellis.
His bare chest pokes through the open V
of his white crossed-over karate shirt.
His belt is black.

Sandra sees him too.
We look at each other and scream briefly,
before turning back to the scene.

Ellis and the other guy bow to the kids,
who bow back.

"I cannot *believe* this," I say.

We watch as they lead the kids through kicks,
jumps, lunges — all that martial arts-type stuff.
Then a little girl crouches to the floor,
and sits, crying.

Ellis sits beside her in the middle of it all,
his large hand on her tiny shoulders,
talking to her.
His gentleness disarms me.

"Oh my god, that's so cute!"
Sandra says.

A moment later, the girl is smiling.
She stands, and Ellis gives her
one more pat on the shoulder.

"I'm dying over here," I say.
"*Dying.*"

We watch for another fifteen minutes,
then decide we need Starbucks.

I've seen everything I need to see
for one night.

Groundhog Day

- Sleep
- Eat (mainly cereal — cornflakes, generally)
- Feel like a giant failure
- Movies with Sandra
- Work with Sandra
- Stalk him
- Think about kissing him
- Avoid Dad
- Worry about Mom

It's like that old movie with
Bill Murray,
where every day is the same,
over and over again,
until he goes cuckoo.

I know
how he felt.

Wednesday

Sandra's parents are at the café tonight.
Mr. and Mrs. Polinsky,
I love them.
They're like another
set of parents to me.

"Mercedes, darling,"
Mrs. Polinsky says,
gathering me in her
cozy arms.
She smells like hand lotion
and cinnamon, always.
Hugs from Mr. Polinsky too,
his eyes crinkling behind his
dark-framed square glasses.

They may not be cool, but they are
all the warmth and safety in the world.

They've come to batch cook for the next week,
make chicken stew and dumplings in vats,
bake pies and strudels and cakes
and freeze everything in those
stainless steel uprights.

I have a whole new appreciation
for the relentlessness of
food service, working here,
but Sandra's parents take it all in stride.

They chat with each other,
laugh and kid as they chop celery,
roll dough and grate carrots.
My parents never laugh and kid with each other,
especially not while they're working.

Later, Sandra's parents sit at a corner table
with cappuccinos, playing gin rummy.
By 7:00 p.m. they're heading home
in their ancient Volvo station wagon.
They'll watch *Homeland*
while Sandra's mom mends a pair of pants
and her dad snores in his chair.

That's their life.
Comfortable, hardworking,
pretty much the same
from day to day.
It seems to work for them.
In some ways it sounds nice.

Sandra sweeps back into the café,
having bought new eyeshadow
at the drugstore next door.

"Polinsky," I say.
"Let's binge-watch Tim Burton movies after work."

Sandra narrows her eyes. "Oh yeah? You don't need to rush home to work on something?"

"Nope!" I say, buoyant.

"We'll start with *Beetlejuice*," she says.

Thursday

The next morning when I wake up, I think:
As if I'm going to school.
It's just one of those days.

Dad's at meetings all day;
Mom's at some yoga thing.
Besides, they never
care if I skip anyway.

The bus and the Skytrain
take me into the city,
a swift 45-minute journey.

I'm faced with its presence
as soon as I exit the station:
The Vancouver Central Gallery.

A lifelong, card-carrying member,
and I haven't been through
its doors in months.
My mom and I used to go
(in between her projects, of course).
We'd talk about the exhibits, have pasta salad
and Perrier in the gallery café afterward.
It was our tradition.

I take a deep breath,
push through the
revolving doors.

TED FRIESEN
the sign greets me as I enter.

The Occupation of Public Space:
Ruminations on Found Objects

That's why I'm here.
It's all for you, Ted.

It's busy,
too busy for a Thursday in January
at 11:00 a.m.

The entrance to the exhibit
is a mash of people,
so I decide
to do it backwards.

It's all there,
everything I love,
everything I've seen in books.

There are his stacks of
vintage suitcases
to resemble the pre-9/11
New York City skyline,

the map of his hometown,
Betsy Layne, Kentucky
(pop. 520, circa 1960),
created with used electronics.

Old cellphones for houses,
streets lined with motherboards.
I turn into the next room,
and there it is.

Celebration of Life,
a tribute to his daughter
Savannah, who passed away
at age four from leukemia.

Stuffed animals —
elephants, rabbits, bears and owls,
sit on six rows of tiny church pews,

each with their head bowed.

My legs weak,
I find a seat.

It's like all of the emotions
I've ever experienced,

joy rage trust anguish
grief hope worry love.

All of the emotions of
everyone in the whole world
swirl around me,
a small sixteen-year-old girl,
with a leather satchel
and corduroy jacket,
sitting on a wooden
art gallery bench.

This is what I've missed.
This is what I love.

Feeling the feels
of art.

Bio, Exhibit Brochure

The works of Ted Friesen, a Kentucky native, have been
heavily influenced by his working-class upbringing in a
small coal town. He explores the intersection of geography
and emotion in his work, using primarily found objects to
create his often large, visceral sculptures. Friesen's work has
been shown in more than fifty countries around the world.
A graduate of Yale and The New School, Friesen is now
based in Vancouver and has recently joined the faculty of
the Wildwood Fine Arts School.

Holy crap.

One of my main talent crushes,
one of my major influences,
is now on the faculty
at Wildwood Fine Arts School.

Ted Friesen.
Ted. Friesen.
TED FRIESEN.
Ted Freaking Friesen!

The Deluxe

I grab a slice of 99-cent pizza,
with all the toppings.
Tomato sauce still likely
crusted on my face,
I make my way through the streets.
Up and down Granville,
past the law courts on Howe,
the fancy hotels on Georgia.

I just need to walk.
It helps me figure things out.

I wasn't going to apply to Wildwood.

For months now that failure,
that fear of future failures,
paralyzed me.
The shame rendered me useless.
I felt like I didn't deserve to try anymore.

By this point I'm taking longer,
more purposeful strides,
my mind raging
like a volcano about to burst.

I want to own that shame.
I want to own that failure.
I want to
OWN IT ALL.

Seeing that art today reignited something in me.
I felt at home in the gallery, more at home
than I do in my own home.

Also: Ted Friesen.

Ted Friesen.

Soon,
I'm running.
People turn to look as I pass.
They probably think I'm late for a bus.

I look up at the clouds and
I feel like I'm running on air,
lighter,
effortless all of a sudden.

I duck around a corner
near the library,
my lungs ablaze.

I pull out my phone

TedFriesenteachesatWildwood
I blurt out,
into my mom's voicemail.

I raise my head,
keep on going.

Home

Mom's at the computer in the kitchen
when I arrive.

"So!" She spins around
in her chair
to face me.
Her eyes have dark hollows
around them.
"Ted Friesen."

"I know!" I squeal.
I can't help myself.

"Does this mean ..."
Mom's eyebrows are raised,
waiting for me to say
what I think she wants me to say.

I nod. "I'm going to try
for it again."

She takes my hands in hers,
looks at me all serious.
"This time, honey,
leave the glue gun out of it."

Surrounded

I remember sitting
on my mom's studio floor
while she worked
(keeping the welding tools
safely at a distance).

I was three, maybe four, and
I'd paw through buckets of
nails, rivets, bolts, screws and
strips of metal that could slice my fingers
if I wasn't careful.
I'd make patterns and curves.
Once I made a river
of nails and metal
that ran from one corner of the studio
to the other,
hundreds of them,
swooping, waving,
in motion,
always in motion.

My mother could have said,
"No, no, don't mess with my things.
Go watch *Sesame Street*."
But she never did.

As long as I didn't bother her,
I could mess with her things
as much as I liked.

Stowell & Co.

My mom says that at age one I gripped
a crayon and sat with a pad of paper for hours,
scribbled on pages and pages.

When I was six
and created elaborate homes for my
beloved My Little Pony collection,
my parents dubbed my bedroom
The Mercedes Stowell Gallery,
showing it off to their friends
at dinner parties.

"An artist, like your mother,"
they'd say,
after swishing up the narrow stairs
in their caftans and silk skirts.

It's like those family businesses
where the dad's a plumber,
and all the kids end up
unplugging drains
when they grow up too —
Smith & Sons, or whatever.

I don't mind, though.
Art's in my blood.
At least I think it is.

On Repeat

In my bedroom that night,
I think about that old Bill Murray
movie again. *Groundhog Day*.

The cycle was finally broken
when he realized
his true purpose in life.

I open my closet door.
I pick up a paintbrush from the pile,
some fabric, a bundle of chewed pencils,
lay them out in front of me.

For the first time in months

I *want* to make art.

Office Hours

The next day,
after school,
I poke my head
through the art room door.

I snuck in,
having been a truant
for the past two days.

Ms. Keyes is there
humming to herself.
(I'm pretty sure it's
something from *Grease*.)
I cross the room until I'm right behind her.
She doesn't hear me.

"Okay," I say,
"I want to do it."

She jumps.
Oil paints and brushes go flying.

Minutes later,
Ms. Keyes has me
sitting on a stool,
tea at my side.

"You want to do the extra assignments?"

"Yeah. And apply to Wildwood."

"What made you decide to —"
She cuts herself off,
shakes her head.
"Never mind.
I'm thrilled."

She clamps
her hands on my knees
and squeezes.

"Ted Friesen is on the faculty,"
I say, not even trying
to hold back my smile.

"I hadn't heard."
She giggles.
"He's very handsome, you know,
in that rugged, denim-shirt sort of way.
I met him once.
He was quite the gentleman."

My mom said the exact same thing.
These artsy middle-aged ladies and
their crushes.

"So? Any ideas?"
Ms. Keyes says,
brushing pencil shavings off
her overalls.

"Not yet," I say,
"but I'm working on it."
My lips are dry and I can't find
my Chapstick in my backpack.

She consults her desk calendar,
flicks up four months' worth of pages.

"A little over fifteen weeks
to go until the application deadline," she says.

Fifteen weeks.

Fifteen weeks to create
the Golden Ticket
that will grant me entry to
my equivalent of

a magical candy factory.

Google

That night,
I swear to myself that
I will work on project ideas.

*Procrastinators prioritize short-term enjoyment
over long-term achievement.*
I hear my mother's voice in my head.

Sitting at my computer, I type in
"Ellis McShay."
It's not like I haven't Googled him before,
but it's always good to do a
re-check.

Apparently there is a rugby player
in Glasgow with the same name.
Lots of scores and game results.
I've seen this dozens of times before,
hoping in vain that he'll be there.
But there's never anything on
my Ellis.

I click to image search
and scroll through
photo after photo of this large red-headed
Scottish rugby player.

Scroll scroll scroll

Page four of images and I'm about to give up,
but then I have an idea.
I type in "Ellis McShay karate."

Bingo.

I click to enlarge the first photo:
Hamilton Karate Stars
the caption says,
from the *Hamilton Daily Star.*

Danny Wilson, Josh Baker and Ellis McShay
swept the provincial championships.

All smiling, arms crossed, black belts around their waists
and medals around their necks.

I click the next one.

It's him,
shirt off,
dark loose pants,
his left leg raised high in a fancy karate kick way.

Naturally I peer closer,
expand the photo to see the
tensed muscles and fierce expression.

Provincial champ Ellis McShay trains for another victory
the caption reads.

I sit back.
My breath leaves my body
like a popped balloon.

x vs. y

Math class.
Algebra.

I have loose sketch paper in my binder
a fresh, sharp 4B pencil
and my perfect subject.

Tuck my legs under me,
tilt my binder between
my lap and my desk.

No one's behind me,
my desk is against the wall,
so I just go for it.

I start at the hair.
Pure black,
dramatic against his pale, pale skin
dotted with freckles.
I sketch quietly
lest it's discovered I'm drawing
his sideburns instead of writing x's and y's.

By the end of the next class
I've completed his profile:
straight nose, fine cheekbones,
eyelashes penciled in
one by one,
high forehead, slight cleft to the chin.

Now I'm working my way
down the torso.
Fangirl that I am,
danged if I'm going to draw
him with a shirt on.

I snort-giggle to myself.
I decide I'll make it kind of ridiculous,
like the cover of
a romance novel.

Time to concentrate.
Through his thin white T-shirt
I can see the taut curve
in his shoulders
when he raises his hand
to offer answers.
He's always right.

I sketch him the way he sits at his desk,
one foot propped up on the desk leg,
one arm leaning forward,
chin in hand.

Perfect neck,
shoulder blades, broad back,
leather belt and jeans.
(I considered pantless,
but let's not get carried away.)

As I'm starting to sketch his fingers
(long and elegant)
Brittany Winters leans over to him,
asks if she can borrow a pencil.

Blast you, Brittany Winters of the
shiny hair and supermodel teeth.

He returns her smile,
his eyes lingering
on her for a moment.

I lose my grip, and
my own pencil clatters to the floor.

He turns, picks it up,
hands it to me,
matter of fact.

No grin.

Sirens

Ellis Emergency
I text Sandra,
when safely around the corner.

"That bitch," she says
five minutes later at our lockers.

"Just ask him out," Sandra says.
"Then all of this analyzing
and pining
and swooning will be over."

I groan. "Who knows, maybe Ellis
likes her. She's hot."

"That's the first time you've ever
actually said his name,"
she says, pretending to look aghast.

"Yeah," I say. "I could only keep
that up for so long."

"But anyhow, Ellis is deeper than that.
I can tell."

"Yeah, but he smiled at *her,*
and not at me."

"You can be pretty intimidating, you know,"
Sandra says, rolling on some lip gloss.
"You know, your whole not-really-talking-
to-other-people thing."

I harrumph.
"Yeah. Okay. Noted."

"Atta girl."
Sandra gives me a quick yet firm
hug, then heads to Home Ec.

Sandra's the best hugger.

22544 Snowdrop Crescent

The familiar green and purple gables
peep out at me through the trees as I round the corner,
home from school.

 "Coolest house ever,"
says anyone who's ever come here.

It's all strange angles and alcoves,
a reading nook here, a corner with built-in bookshelves
there,
a massive studio to one side to hold
all the welding my mother could muster, and
an office space next to it
for my father to spend approximately
twenty-three hours a day in.

The house is filled with antiques,
African masks,
puppets from the Czech Republic,
whose porcelain heads lean demurely to one side.
I always imagined they came alive at night,
dancing among the bookshelves and crannies
that overflowed with paintbrushes and curios.

The bathroom is Mona Lisa everything:
wallpaper towels figurines mirror frame.
Everyone loves it.

The tower
was a guest bedroom until I was born,
and my dad loves to tell me who it housed:
Gathie Falk, Jeff Wall, Douglas Coupland,
stopping by on their way out of town.
(He's a real name-dropper.)

My mother wanted this funny little piece of land
because of the street name
and its proximity to the river.

Nothing bad could ever happen
when you live on Snowdrop Crescent,
she told my father all those years ago.

Dessert

On the kitchen table,
a note:
Doctor's appointment.
See you later.
Love, Mom.

I feel my shoulders relax with relief.
She's finally going.

She's been having blurred vision,
more headaches, so many headaches,
nausea,
and that "one pesky seizure."
Maybe low iron, she figures,
possibly mononucleosis.

My mother never even
gets colds.
Strong constitution, she says.

I just want her better.

I make chocolate pudding
with Cool Whip on top
because I feel like it.

Afterward, I dollop
some into a bowl for her.

A Post-It note
stuck to the cling-wrapped top:

In the mood for
a petroleum product?

Gut Bomb

I'm in the kitchen later for some water.
My dad is there,
licking chocolate remnants
off his big fingers.

"I made that for *Mom*."

His phone bleeps. Without pause,
he answers it,
waves away my comment
like it's a mosquito.

I stand in the doorway and stare
at the back of his pudgy head for a while.

I haven't told him I'm going to
apply to Wildwood again.
What's the point, anyway?
He's just going to think
I'll screw it up again.

Fine Arts Business Magazine, October 2010

CANADA'S MOST UNLIKELY ART DEALER

To meet Paul Stowell, you'd never guess you're talking to
the wunderkind of Canadian sculpture deals. A former
gallery owner, the Vancouver native walks with the swagger
of a car salesman and has a penchant for bacon and onion
potato chips, which he offers me in his home office in Maple
Ridge, BC. With a singing plastic fish mounted on the wall
and other lowbrow tchotchkes on his shelves, Stowell looks
like he could be selling you your next used Toyota. But with
a BFA in Visual Art, an MBA from the London School of
Economics and a staggering track record of sales in sculpture
and public art, Paul Stowell is undeniably the real thing.

"I was into painting in university," Stowell says when asked
how he got into his line of work. "Abstracts, bright colours,
that sort of thing. My wife got me into sculpture. And then
in second year I took a business class in marketing, and I
was gonzo from there."

He pauses, thoughtfully chewing on a handful of potato
chips. Crumbs decorate the front of his black Pink Floyd
T-shirt. He doesn't wipe them off. "I read everything I could
on being an art dealer. I tracked careers and sales. And then
I offered to sell the work of every Vancouver artist I loved.
Sure, I lived on peanut butter sandwiches some months. But
it didn't take long before I had something going on. Galleries
would call me, asking what was new. I had a roster of private
clients whose homes I'd fill with art."

Stowell chuckles and shakes his head, reaching for another handful of chips. At forty, he runs Stowell Fine Art and travels regularly to the US, Europe and Asia, where he brokers high-profile deals.

His business associates agree that Stowell's unusual approach is welcome in the often uber-serious contemporary art community.

"Paul's real," says Kristen Denby, director of collections for the Vancouver Central Gallery. "In this world of pretense, he's a breath of fresh air. And he's got the best laugh in the business."

Stephen Wilks, head curator for the Simon Fraser Museum of Art, echoes Denby's sentiments. "Paul's my go-to person for anything related to modern sculpture. He knows all the hot new artists from around the world, and he's got a great sense for trends. He's a rare gift to the art world."

Stowell also manages the career of his wife, Canadian sculptor Patrice Stowell, whose most recent work, *Treasure Trove*, was purchased in a seven-figure deal by the city of Ljubljana, Slovenia.

"Patrice and I met in university," Paul says, looking at a smiling photo of himself, his wife and their young daughter on his desk. "Our eyes met across a crowded art studio, and the rest is history." Stowell gives one of his signature chuckles and then takes another frame off the wall.

Art, it seems, runs in the family. His daughter is also a gifted painter and sculptor. "Now here's a young artist to watch." He chuckles again. "She may only be seven years old, but she's a force to be reckoned with. Last year she discovered Andy Goldsworthy and fell in love. Spent weeks last summer putting this together."

In the frame is a photograph, which Paul proudly displays to me with a flourish. Laid out on a lawn, it's the outline of the front of a house, made of doll legs and arms, mixed with branches and sticks. A small "garden" of more doll arms and legs is stuck into a square patch of dirt next to the house shape. Even to my jaded eyes, it's stunning. Stowell's daughter, Mercedes, stands beside it, her eyes squinting as she smiles, just like her father.

Stowell carefully replaces the frame on the wall and turns back to me. "Art is a huge part of my family's identity," he says. "I'm very grateful for that, and proud."

To learn more about Paul Stowell and the artists he represents, visit www.stowellfineart.com.

— Jane Dixon, Western Division reporter

Right Angles

Mr. Beadle moved the desks around.
Now we're in groups of four
two desks, side by side,
facing each other.

I'm the last person to class
and there's only one spot left
at a group of desks
with Jeb,
Jessie, president of the chess club,
and ... guess who.

Brittany Winters is off in some other
group in the corner. Good.

The seat is right next to Ellis.
So close that our shoulders might touch.

I can't move.

The whole class looks at me
still standing in the doorway.

"Miss Stowell," Mr. Beadle says
in his drawling British accent,
"Are you delivering pizza,
or are you going to take your seat?"

There are a few snickers
as I make my way to my desk.
I hope I remembered to put on deodorant.

Mr. Beadle hands out worksheets,
explains that we're to complete them with our
"next-door neighbours."
I look at Ellis,
the boy next door.

It's geometry.
I suck at geometry.

The worksheet has
a couple of triangles on it and
something about the
Hypotenuse-Leg Theorem.

What values of a and b make $\triangle IJK \cong \triangle DCE$?

I shift in my seat.
He's going to think I'm dumb
because I have no freaking clue.

I can feel his spicy warmth.
This is the closest we've ever been.

He's already got his eyes on the sheet,
pencil not twirling,
filling in the blanks
with perfect assuredness.

This gives me a strange little moment to
analyze his features further.
His dad is Japanese?
Other than the black hair
I don't see it.

"Um, what's the Hypotenuse-Leg Theorem?"
Jessie whispers across the desks.
I feel better.
I'm not the only dummy at the table.

"Two right triangles are congruent
if and only if the hypotenuse and
a leg of one right triangle
are congruent to the hypotenuse and
a leg of the other right triangle,"
Ellis says, spinning his pencil.

Jessie stares at him, eyebrows knitted, mouth open.

Miss Stowell, I think, hiding my smile in my scarf,
I do believe your boy is a bit of a nerd.

Triangle Inequality Theorem

"Do you want to do these ones,
and I'll do these?"
he says in a low voice, pointing to
a column of questions about triangles.

"I'm going to be honest with you,"
I whisper,
attempting to make eye contact,
then glancing back at the paper.
"I'm not very good at geometry.
But I love patterns."

As soon as I say it, I hear
Sandra's voice in my head:
You DORK.

My fingers brush my binder cover
to which I've glued a photo of
Nils-Udo's *Summer in the Park*,
and I hope he notices.

He sighs, slides the worksheet over to his desk,
starts filling in the answers.

Crap. Now he thinks I'm one of those
group members who doesn't
do anything.

Too late now. He's totally focused.

February 14

I hate this day anyway,
but in my delusional brain,
Ellis and I were going to be
hating it together.

That night, as we're closing up the café,
Sandra says,
"Odin's Sire's playing an
all-ages show at the
Pitt Meadows Hall tonight.
Anti-Valentine's Day.
Let's go."

I hate Odin's Sire's music.
But I'm not going to tell
Sandra that, since her boyfriend, Carl, is,
after all,
the lead singer and main lyricist.
I try to make up an excuse about
watching a documentary with my mom,
but she's not having it.

Next thing I know —
because that's how it always
goes with Sandra —
I'm in her passenger seat,
driving to the
next town over.

"We're totally on the guest list, of course," Sandra says.

Well, at least that's something.

The Gig Is Up

It might be Anti-Valentine's,
but the second Sandra sees Carl
it seems pretty lovey-dovey to me.

Carl's a nice enough guy,
Grade 12, long wavy brown hair,
jean vest, shitkicker boots.
Sandra has always had
a soft spot for metalheads.

I stand to the side, as usual,
awkward. Carl at last departs
to tune his guitar.

The place starts to fill up with
mostly Pitt Meadows kids. They've got
their Friday night finery on:
plaid shirts, boots, tight tank tops.

The entire time in my head I'm going
whyamIherewhyamIherewhyamIhere

and then I notice a guy standing next to me.

"Hi," the guy says.
I look up. Tall. Blond hair sticking
out from under a Vancouver Canucks cap.
Big nose. Good smile.

"Hi," I say, not sure why he's talking to me.

"I've never seen you at
a show before," he says.
He sticks out his hand. "Steve."

I shake it. Big palm, stubby fingers.
"I'm just here with my friend.
Her boyfriend's in the band."

"Nice. Grab you a drink?
There's nothing too exciting here,
but I saw some Jones soda."

Sandra sidles over after Steve goes off
in search of pop. She's been watching.

"Dude! That cute guy is totally
hitting on you."

Shivers crackle up my arms,
down my spine.
Not in a good way.

"What do I do?"

"Better think fast," she says,
heading back to the front of the stage,
"he's coming this way."

Like the super-suave gal that I am,
I turn and run out the side door.

Odin's Sire's opening chords drone
through the metal panels.
Good, I think, *maybe now he'll be distracted.*

I hide around the corner. A couple of
girls finish their smokes, say hi as they
pass me, then head in the side door.

I watch the winter air steam
into curls in front of my face
as I exhale heavily.

My nose is freezing. I stomp
my feet, which are quickly
losing any sensation.

Why do I let Sandra drag me
to these things?

Why?

The side door swings open.
All I see is the silhouette of a
ball cap brim.

It's Steve, cream soda still in hand.

"What the hell," I hear him say,
then the door shuts again.

I don't want to go back in,
but I won't last long out here
in my thin cardigan.

Ugh.

Ten Below Zero

Odin's Sire is known
for their epic shows.
They're only five songs in
as far as I can tell
from outside,
fifteen more to go.

And their songs aren't short.

The door bangs open again.
I hear the soft clump of
sneakers down the steps.

Two voices,
male,
around the corner.

"Yeah, they've got a load
of Norse mythology references in
their songs," one says.

"That one about Loki was
pretty decent." The other voice,
deeper than the first one.

"You here with Brittany?"

"I guess."

"Good job, man, good job."

I know those voices.
Both of them, especially
the second one.
Ellis.

This is ridiculous.
Completely ridiculous.

"Valkyries carry the slain ..."
To Valhalla, on the plain ..."

Ellis and Jeb are
singing Odin's Sire lyrics
in guttural growls.

I review my current situation.
I'm still in my work skirt,
bare legs, ballet flats,
tank top, cardigan,
hiding in the shadows behind a
community hall with an all-ages
death metal show going on inside.

Ellis is allegedly here
with Brittany Winters.
Maybe that's okay because
he's singing death metal with
a total idiot.

And I'm trapped, a thicket of
blackberry brambles
behind me.

My Lungs, They Betray Me

Before I can muffle it with my sleeve,
I cough. Fortunately, Ellis and Jeb are now
grunting another song,
so they don't hear me.

Two seconds later, though,
a figure lunges,
peers around the corner.
It's Ellis.

I back up. Thorns tug at my sweater.
Ouch.

"Oh hey."
A large hand grasps my arm,
pulls me into the light.
His hand. My arm.
His fingers wrap
all the way around.

He's touching my arm.

"What are you doing back there?"

My jaw is locked from cold.
"Freezing my ass off,"
I manage to say,
through gritted teeth.

Ellis laughs. I've never heard him
laugh before. It comes from deep inside
his chest.

I'm not sure I've forgiven him
for the singing, though.
Or being here with Brittany Winters.

Jeb doesn't even acknowledge my existence.
"They're back on, man. Let's head."

Ellis makes no move
toward the door.

"So you actually *like* Odin's Sire?"
I still have a hard time saying
their name without laughing.

Ellis looks at me like I have
several heads. "Uh, *yeah*." Dead serious.

I could pretend I like them too.
But I don't.
 "My best friend's boyfriend is in the band.
That's why I'm here."

"Really? That's dope."

Ellis turns to look up at the building,
all white wood siding and interesting angles.
"Cool building," he says.

"It used to be a church," I say.

"Explains the good acoustics," he says.
"We didn't have as many modern
builds in Ontario. A lot more old buildings."

He pauses.
"You still didn't tell me why you're out here,
freezing your ass off."

I explain my situation.
Maybe it'll make him jealous.

He sucks in a breath. "Ooh, I would never
run away from a Jones cream soda."

I wrap my arms around myself.
"I'd rather have a hot chocolate right now,
to be honest."

"And if I'm honest," he says,
"I don't really like Odin's Sire.
Maybe just for the humour factor."

Relief floods me. Almost enough to
warm me up a little. But not quite.

"So, you're into, um, buildings and stuff?"

He laughs.
"I am, yes."

"Like Hundertwasser.
Saw it on your binder."
I pray that this does not
make me sound like
Crazy Stalker Girl.

He says, "You know
about Hundertwasser?"

"My family's into that kind of stuff.
My dad saw Hundertwasserhaus
in Vienna two years ago."

Ellis leans against the white wood siding.
"I've never met anyone else who knows
what that quote is about," he says.

I feel a little warmer
all of a sudden.

"What's your favourite building?" I ask.

"The —" he starts to say.

"Ellis. Tadashi. McShay,"
someone calls from
the top of the steps.

It's Brittany.
I jolt at the sight. How does she know
his middle name, anyway?
She's totally nosey.

She probably straight-out
asked him so that she could have
an enticing piece of information
about him that no one else has.

"I've been waiting inside for you forever,"
she says to Ellis, tossing her hair,
stroking his upper arm. I imagine his warmth.
I wonder how she could so casually
touch Ellis like that.
This always seems so easy for other girls.

"Oh hi," she says to me, then gives me a twice-over.
"You look *frozen* in your waitress clothes."
To Ellis: "Come on. They're about to do
the one about Thor."

As *if* Brittany actually likes this band.
Biggest Taylor Swift fan there is.

"In a minute," he says.

"Whatever," she says,
tossing her hair again.
(Do girls like Brittany take lessons
in that?)
She turns on her heel and
then she's through the side door.

In a minute.
Ellis McShay just said
in a minute to Brittany Winters.

I cannot *wait* to tell Sandra.

"Be right back," he says.
And goes inside.

Five minutes later
he returns,
presses a small Styrofoam cup
into my hand.

The steam reaches my nose.
Hot chocolate.

"The Dancing House," he says.
"Czech Republic.
Google it."

He winks, jogs up the steps
and is gone.

Entry

"He's an enigma," Sandra says
on the way home.

"And he winked at me,"
I say.

"I didn't think anyone under the age of
seventy-five winked anymore,"
Sandra says.

We both shrug, and at the same time
laugh-shout:
"Enigma!"

At home, I open Google.
The Dancing House, or Fred and Ginger,
is the nickname given to the Nationale-Nederlanden
building on the Rašínovo nábřeží in Prague,
Czech Republic, Wikipedia tells me.

It's not what I expected.

I thought the Guggenheim, maybe, or
the Chrysler Building,
but this is a nice surprise.

Quirky and asymmetrical,
like a cartoon character
or something from
a Tim Burton film.

It looks like it's alive.
A deconstructivist masterpiece,
someone's written about it.

I love it.

Grey

Monday
in math class
the desks are in the same formation.

Being creatures of habit
(as Mr. Beadle likes to say),
we all sit in the same seats,
which means I'm next to Ellis again.

I wore a new dress with cat heads on it and
my suede ankle boots
for the occasion.

"Hey," he says,
smiles at me
as I sit down.
His eyes crinkle,
the same grey as his T-shirt
the same grey as the sky.

I came prepared.

"The Dancing House," I say,
nodding my approval.
"Nice lines. Full of quirk."

"Perfect in its imperfection,"
he says with that
broad, wonderful grin.

Smooth Move

My week revolves around
math class.

Wednesday,
geometry again,
with my favourite neighbour.

I'm supposed to be finding
all points of intersection of the circle
$x^2 + 2x + y^2 + 4y = -1$
(whatever that means), and then
my pencil slides out of my hand,
slips down the desk to the floor.

I lean over the metal side bar of the desk,
bump my binder as I do,
and it flips over,
everything,
onto the floor.

I watch like it's in slow motion.
The sketch of
Sexy Ellis
flutters out, lands on top.

Jeb grabs it before I do.

"Well, well,"
he says, holding it away
from my grasping hands.
"What have we here?"

He turns around the room
like a kindergarten teacher
showing the illustrations in a book,
giving everyone a good view.
I'm whisper-shouting, *"Noooooo!"*
Jeb's chortling.
Jessie's looking at me
with sympathetic eyes.

Laughter spreads like
terrible birdsong through the classroom.

"I gotta say, Stowell," Jeb says.
"You have some *skills*.
Look at the definition in those lats."
I hate Jeb.

Mr. Beadle intervenes,
is decent enough to roll up the sketch
and place it in his desk drawer.

I can't look up. I can't even.
Not in Ellis's direction.
I'm sitting slouched now,
hiding behind my textbook
propped up on my desk.

If this happened to Sandra
she'd just slough it off,
laugh harder than everyone else,
make it a joke.
But I'm not like that.

Ellis isn't laughing
like the rest of them,
but I can see in my peripheral vision
that his ears are red.

I slouch farther down behind my book
because I don't know what else to do.
Geometric formulas swim blurry
over my corneas.

Evening Shift

I debrief with Sandra
on the way to the café.
She agrees about the gravity
of the current situation.

"Don't worry, we'll think of something,"
she says, donning her apron and
hairnet in the back room.

Just then, my phone buzzes in my pocket.

Another One

We need you.
Now.

Text from Dad.
I start texting him back, and
it buzzes again.
Now he's calling me.

"Your mom had a seizure,"
Dad says, yelling from his car's Bluetooth.

Oh no. Not another one.

"She didn't come to for ten minutes.
By then she was already
in the back of the ambulance."

I should tell him. I should tell him about the other one.

"Mercedes! You there?"

"Yeah." My voice is a whisper.

"You at work? I'm coming to get you."

My phone slips from my hands and onto the prep counter
as an earthquake shudders through me.

Mom.

The Unknown

My father is brisk, all business
when he picks me up.
He tells me that they want to
keep her overnight for observation,
conduct tests.

"Your mom will bounce back,"
he says, patting my knee. "She always does."

He chuckles,
slurps his drive-through coffee.

The corner of his right eye
twitches until he presses it
with his index finger.

Mrs. Stowell

"Mrs. Stowell"
the young nurse calls her.
My mom giggles —
it's weak, but still a giggle.
"Mrs. Stowell doesn't suit me,"
she says.

Neither does this clanging metal bed
or baggy blue hospital gown
or how thin her legs look
under the white sheet.

The whole scene is wrong,
the most wrong thing I've ever seen.
I want to pick her up and take her home.
I want to be around the kitchen table again.

My father sits
on one of the green vinyl chairs,
pinching the bridge of his nose,
phone in hand (like always),
eyes closed.

All I can think is:
My mom has some freaky medical problem.

Also: *I've ruined my chances with my
no-longer-future-boyfriend.*

What the bloody hell.

I get some quarters from my dad
for a Coke Zero,
go around the corner
and stare at the hospital floor
for a while.

Thursday, 1:00 p.m.

When I finally wake up the next day
my first thought is:
I can't let love distract me.

It's probably a good thing
that my clumsy self
destroyed my chance at love.

Let him go, I think,
let him go,
black belt and swoony eyes and all.

You have art to think about.
You have Mom to think about.

I get that stiletto-heel kick in my chest,
hunch over and
wrap my arms around myself
momentarily
before I shake it off.

Texts

Tests inconclusive
Still at hospital
Dad.

You okay??
LAOSPT, S

Mercedes-love,
Don't worry.
I'm okay.

I love you.
- Mom.

CALL ME!
Sandra.

I take my phone,
turn it off with one hard poke,
toss it into my boot on the floor.

I'm not going to talk to anyone today
and possibly not tomorrow
or the next day or the next.

Mercedes' Brain Map

35% What the hell is wrong with Mom?
30% Ellis's cheekbones.
    (stop it stop it stop it)
25% Ted Freaking Friesen!
10% random song lyrics and '80s movie lines.
0% artistic inspiration.

Working Not Working

Coffee
toast with butter
Wildwood Fine Arts School brochure
propped against the vase of drooping gerberas on the table.

I stare at it.
I hold my chin in my hands.

All those weeks to go.
It feels like forever but
I know from past experience
that it's not.

I punch my head
right in the middle of my forehead,
trying to make it work.

Five minutes later
(head whacking having proved ineffective)
pajamas still on
(old yoga pants and Vampire Weekend T-shirt)
I'm tromping around the yard,
talking to myself like a crazy person.

Near a pile of wood pieces
I barf up my coffee and toast.

I lurch,
hunched over for a time.

I contemplate the two-by-fours;
one knotty piece —
sanded, maybe as long as my forearm —
catches my attention.

48 Hours Later

Sunday at 2:00 p.m.
equals
Mercedes Stowell,
still clad in stench-riddled
Vampire Weekend T-shirt and yoga pants
in her backyard,
surrounded by
138 pieces of two-by-four,
varying in length,
stacked around her in a hexagon.
She sits in the centre of it all
twirling her hair
eyes glazed over.

I talk like this in my head.
Third person.
In a voice like a BBC reporter,
as though they're standing there with a
microphone, reporting with me in the background.

Mom's at the hospital for more tests.
I haven't been to school since Wednesday.

These stacks of wood are all I have right now.

Monday

Three hours at the hospital last night:
more tests
test after test
she's going for another MRI.

Last night I sat
on the edge of her bed
looking at *Cosmo* and *Glamour*
with her
because what else are you going to do
when that's all the hospital has?

Even though neither of us ever reads that garbage.

House/Home

Mom is home now, resting.
The house feels better with her in it;
the walls seem to sigh with relief.

Dude

It takes me a while to hear it:
"Dude? Dude?"

Finally I look up
from my stacks of wood,
buckets of nails and
canvas pieces strewn everywhere.

She's unmistakable,
a charcoal outline
backed by the late-afternoon
Tuesday sun.
Broad shoulders, broad hips,
it's her:

a venti chocolate chip frappuccino in each hand,
my best friend.

"What is going on?"
she says.
"Where have you been? You missed
work last night. My mom had to cover."

"I'm sorry," I say.

She surveys the scattered wood pieces,
my dirty clothes.

"What are you *doing*?"

"I don't know exactly," I say.
"I felt like making something."

"Come on," she says.
"Twizzlers and *The Breakfast Club*
at my place.
Forget all this for a while."

Without arguing, I follow.
There's so much I need to tell her.

Warm Glow

In the comfortable yellow
of Sandra's TV room,
at the triumphant end of
The Breakfast Club,
I get that desolate feeling again.
That overwhelming worry.

"Sandra," I say,
my voice cracking.
"My mom might be sick.
They don't know what's
wrong with her."

"What's happening?" Sandra says,
leaning toward me.

I tell her about the tests and the headaches
and the seizure and the everything.

Sandra pauses, thoughtful. "My aunt had
something like that a while ago.
Turned out to be a virus.
Besides, your mom's basically invincible."

I nod and flop back on the couch,
feeling a slight sense of relief.

Invincible.
Maybe Sandra's right.

Wednesday

The school has called,
wondering when I'm coming back.

Today, Mom says.

Classes

Doodling in my binder in history,
I might have something
resembling an idea
for my Wildwood project.

That afternoon in math
I barely remember
myself from the
week previous.

But they haven't forgotten.

On my desk is a photo of a
beefy man from a
firefighter calendar,
with Ellis's head glued on top
of the guy's thick neck.

Jesus.
I slap the picture off the desk,
crumple it in my binder.
"Saving it for later?" Jeb says,
snorting with laughter.
He's never forgiven me
for that time in seventh grade
when I told Jenny Morrison
(beautiful ballerina Jenny Morrison,
whose father played for the
Vancouver Canucks)

that weaselly little Jeb Lloyd liked her,
and she made him a laughingstock for months.
I slide into my seat.
Jessie gives my arm a pat
and Ellis isn't even there.

But nothing affects me now.
I've got the armour of creativity around me,
and the protection of worry.
Everything else is
so small and stupid.

As Mr. Beadle starts going over integers,
Ellis brushes in late
(he's never late).
Even in my mental state I see his
baggy pale jeans and bright green sweater
with a googly-eyed felt moose on it.

He sits down next to me,
clears his throat.

Across the desks, Jeb mouths,
"Dude, what the hell?"
Flicking his fingers up and down
over Ellis's sartorial choice.

I look again.

Yeah, WTF?

At Home

Surrounded by my two-by-fours again,
I think of Ellis.

The ugly moose sweater,
the loose wrong-colour jeans.
It seemed like a grandma outfit.

No one cared about whatever I'd done
as soon as he walked in.

He baffles me.
The entire situation baffles me.

I turn back to my wood pieces,
back to my idea.

Miss Haney

Mixed media
Wood, iron, vinyl, cloth

A feminist commentary on societal attitudes toward beauty
and the "building" of a media-ready image. Just as celebrities
are constructed to match society's expectations, so is this
ten-foot-tall beauty queen, featuring a bouquet of rebar and
tin flowers, and a body made from reclaimed pine.

Shoe In?

Once I've written it down,
committed to it,
I don't think
I just *do*.

I assemble my stacks of wood,
arranged according to length,
pile my tools — hammer, screwdriver, level, saw,
buckets of nails and screws.

I start at the bottom,
saw off three inches of board,
hammer on a straight piece,
make bows out of reflective tape.

Two hours later
I line up the high heels.
And gasp a little because
they're perfect.

Beauty standards commentary
+ reclaimed materials
+ feminism
= Wildwood Fine Arts School admissions jury wet dream.

Right?

Pillow Talk

It's weird,
my mom lying in bed like this.
Under the covers I see her knees twitch
up and down.
She's never still,
but it's doctor's orders.

I accidentally bounce on the edge
of the mattress, but
she doesn't seem to mind.
I describe the recycled wood,
the social commentary,
the feminist slant.

She listens, pauses
for a long, long time,
puts her fingers to her lips in thought.

"Interesting,"
she says, finally.

"What?" I say, my heart dropping a little.
"Don't you like it?"

"It's just that it's
so different for you, honey."

This was not the reaction
I was hoping for.

"No it's not," I say,
too loud.

"I mean, I'm thrilled about the
feminist theme,"
she says,
"but I didn't think that was a
big interest of yours."

She touches my cheek with
the back of her thin hand.
I shake my head, shake it off,
even though I know I shouldn't
because she's ill
with god knows what.

"Of course it's something I care about," I say.
"I'm working really hard on it."

"Okay," she says,
"that's wonderful, then."

Breathe In

Past midnight
I march out to my wood stacks,
hammer together a leg
but smash my thumb.

I tie a scrap of canvas around it
and keep hammering
under the stars.

I love the rhythm of
wood nail hammer nail
wood nail hammer nail.

Mercredi

I hear his footsteps behind me
on the way to Madame George's
French 11 class.
They sound like sneakers.
Tsubos.
The purple ones.

I don't know how I know it,
I just do.

"How are you?"
he says,
slightly breathless
from catching up to me.

"Me?"
I say like an idiot,
looking up from his shoes.

"Yes, you," he says,
his grin taking up half his face with
slightly too-large shiny teeth.

He's like a big golden firefly
buzzing alongside me,
and I don't know
what to do about it.

"Fine," I say,
again like an idiot.

It's our first interaction since The Drawing.
It's like embarrassment and glee
and surprise have been put in a blender
and set to frappe.
I seriously have no idea what to say.

"I just wanted to see how you are," he says.
"Sorry Jeb's a jerk."
He pauses. "Jenny Morrison. He told me."

"That asshole," I say, before
I can stop myself.

He laughs, a head-tipped-back sort of laugh.

"Don't worry about the drawing. I liked it.
Slightly creepy, but flattering.
Maybe I should work out more."

Once again,
I'm mortified.

No, you're perfect, I want to say.
But instead I choke out "Thanks."

The class buzzer
echoes down the hall.

"See you soon," he calls,
that warm laugh still
in his voice
as he heads toward the gym.
Then he turns back
for one and two and three seconds,
and smiles.

Snack Shack

Meet me at the SS at lunch,
I text Sandra.

I'm ripping at the seams
like a doll with my stuffing coming out.

Egg Salad

Sandra shares her lunch with me
because I forgot to bring mine,
or any money.
It doesn't matter anyway
because I can only muster a nibble.

We go over and over
the story of Ellis tracking me
down in the hallway,
me being an idiot.
I wonder aloud why he would
go to all the trouble of doing that.

Sandra says,
"He seems pretty into you."

Nothing More Than Feelings

Tumour.
Large but likely treatable.
Chemotherapy, radiation,
possibly an operation.
A *brain operation*.
"Cautiously optimistic,"
the doctors say.

Back at home,
my parents ask how I'm feeling,
ask me how I'm doing.
It's like the hospital
gave them a "cancer talk" pamphlet
and they're reading from it.
My mom is surprisingly calm,
given it's her brain they're talking about.

I can't think,
don't know what to think.
I run upstairs,
take solace on my rooftop gable.

Later I'll text Sandra,
but for now,
I'll just be alone.

Fallout

I feel like I shouldn't go to school
but for some reason, I do.
Everything's a fuzz of people
and clanging lockers,
and it's all too much.

Sandra finds me at my locker, runs to me,
hugs me like she'll never let go.
We skip biology and French,
wander around the woods
behind the school and
throw stones in the
muck of the pond there.

Ms. Keyes beckons me to her office after school.
Word has already gotten around.

"I'm sorry about your mother's illness,"
she says, two deep lines between her eyebrows.
Hugs me.
"I wish that would change the deadline," she goes on,
"but it doesn't."

After school I want to run to Sandra's and
watch *Sixteen Candles* with her,
forget about everything for two hours,
but I promised I'd go to

my mom's first chemotherapy session.

Port of Entry

My mom looks down at her thin arms,
at the translucent tube running
from the IV stand down into her hand.
Yesterday they put a port there
to easily insert the tube, week after week.
Her hands are for welding metal,
not permanent points of entry
for cancer drugs.

"Pretty surreal, hey?" she says,
watching the medicine
drip drip drip.

More than surreal.
It's the most wrong
thing I've ever seen.
I squirm in my vinyl seat,
next to her.

"Oh, hon," my mom says,
rubbing my leg with her free hand.
"I shouldn't have dragged you here."

I'm gripped with the need to tell her,
suddenly. About Ellis.
We'll be here for two hours.
Might as well talk about something
interesting.

"Mom," I blurt, "there's a boy.
I like him. He might like me too."

"Reeeeaaaallly,"
she says,
sitting up a little.

I tell her about Ellis,
and Hundertwasser,
about that bloody
picture I drew.
"Noooo!" she chortles.

I tell her about the hallway chat,
his crinkly grin,
the *see you soon*.
"But I feel bad," I say,
looking down at my lap.
"Because of all *this*."
I wave my hand across the treatment room.

Mom smiles.
"I'm happy for the distraction,
to be honest.
I think it's wonderful.
Sounds like you're
on the right track there, Mercedes."

She looks back up at the tube.
Drip drip drip.
"I hope I am too.

"Because I want to kick
this stupid tumour's *ass*."

But Then

That night
after her treatment
Mom's in her studio,
Dad's in his office.

Everything's different,
but nothing has changed.

I head outside,
bang wood together for a while.

Mom and I hadn't talked like
that in months,
like we did today at the hospital.
I missed that ease, the
girlfriend talk,
we used to have in these
in-between days.
The space of time
after one project and
before the next.

Except that before today
it was never in a treatment room,
surrounded by IV stands
and nurses
and inspirational posters.

Now I want even
more to please her
by ripping my knuckles open over
these rusty nails and rotten planks.

I want to see the golden flecks
glow in her eyes again.

If I don't,
I'll be a mess.
If I don't,
it just might kill me.

Friday

"I'm going to apply
to Wildwood again," I say,
looking into my mug,
at the cream swirling into clouds.

Sandra stands up from
wiping the tables.

"I thought you gave up on that."
Her voice is louder than it needs to be.

I shrug. "I thought I did too. But
that piece you saw me working on,
all the boards and nails?
It could be something."

"But you said you weren't going to re-apply."

"I know, I know,"
I say.
"But I have my reasons to try again."

I start to tell her about my idea
the feminist slant
the recycled wood
but she's clanking plates around
in the kitchen,
not even listening.

"Listen, I've got a bunch of stuff
to do back here. See you tomorrow."

I know that rise in Sandra's voice,
that hoarse edge she gets when
she's annoyed.

I know she's annoyed.
She wants everything to stay as it is,
and maybe now,
it won't.

I leave from the side door,
grab a brownie on my way out.

Relentless

In history class
I sit, as usual, with my left leg
crossed over my right,
which lately has taken
to shaking, uncontrollable.

"Aggressive neoadjuvant treatments,"
the doctors said,
which means that they're trying
to shrink the tumour
before surgery.

It sounds too strange
and impossible to comprehend:
Before surgery.

Before they take
my mother's beautiful head
and split it wide open.

My fingernails are stubs.
I don't care
who started World War II,
or who ended it.
It's all the past.
All I care about is the present.
The future? That's something
I don't want to think about
right now.

Folding

Math class.
On my desk
in intricate creasings of brown paper:
a cow, maybe,
or a deer.

I flick it around in my fingers,
glance around the room.

Ellis isn't sitting next to me today.
He's across the room helping
Jake Mitchell with his algebra.

I put the paper creature in my pocket,
keep my hand over it lightly.

Wunderbar

I see Sandra at the Snack Shack,
show her the paper animal thing,
not sure if she's still pissed at me
(we didn't talk all weekend).

She flicks it back and forth in her fingers
the same way I did.

"What is it?" I say.

"It's a moose," she says, like I'm stupid.
"I can tell by the antlers.
I saw a real one up north once."

"What do you think it means?"
I say, taking it back.

"It means Ellis made you a paper moose,"
she says, her voice dry.

"It was him, wasn't it?"

Sandra snorts.
"Moose sweater. Moose origami.
Who else would it be, dummy?"
She turns and stalks off,
her boot heels clomping
down the hall.

Nope. Not forgiven yet.

Unfolding

The moose stays in my pocket
all day
through biology and English Lit.
I touch its thin ears as I read Ophelia's lines
in *Hamlet*.

Later, at home
on my stomach, on the floor,
pillow under my chest,
I toss the moose between my palms.

Looking closely,
I see pen marks on its underside.
I peel back a thin layer of its nose.
The brown paper rips a little.
I follow the creases —
One antler, then the other
unfold unfold unfold
until I have an open square
with writing on it — blue ballpoint pen.

555 312 4090

Contact

Oh my god.
It's his number.

I fall on my bed,
the paper clasped
against my heart.

Then I think of Mom,
vomiting and weak from
treatments.
I feel guilty being all swoony
right now.

But then I remember she said,
I think it's wonderful.

And it is.
If only I knew
what I should do.

Paused

I pace
around my room
look out my window.

The piles of wood
are going slimy in the rain.
My masterpiece on hold
after the initial fireworks.

I really want to talk to Sandra,
but it's too soon.
She needs her time.

I think about texting him,
but don't know what to say that would be
brilliant and witty enough.

Finally, I heave myself on my bed and
fall asleep, clothes on.

Later

You're lucky I looked inside
is all I text him
when I wake in a daze at 10:00 p.m.

I wait, barely breathing,
check my phone every two seconds.

One hour later:

I figured yr pretty clever.

Do you stay up late a lot?

Yep. Night owl. U?

Yeah, a lot. What do you do up late? Sorry, bad question?

LOL. Read draw video games, whatevs. U?

I mainly just do tortured artist things.

1:00 a.m.
I'm sitting on my roof now. Like I told you about.

U still havnt told me abt your art.

Okay, Ellis, before we go any further. There's something you need
to know about me.

??

I hate text shorthand. And emojis. Mega pet peeve.

What are you, like 65? I'm sorry if I offended you.

Now you know.

I really want to write LOL but I won't.

Thanks, I appreciate that.

2:00 a.m.

Are you still on the roof?

Yes, but I might go in. Getting cold.

I wish I was there.

I wish you were too.

I could come over ...

NOOOOOOO! We can't.

shrug Can't blame me for trying.

Even though of course,
more than anything,
I want Ellis to be up on this gable with me.

I can't believe this is
happening.

I can't believe that Ellis McShay
just texted *I wish I was there*
to ME.

I don't know how to do this.

911

And then
sirens
red and white lights
flash
in the driveway.

Gotta go. Sorry.

I climb in my bedroom window,
skid into the hall
and down the stairs.

Mom's on the floor of their bedroom,
body tensed and quaking,
eyes rolled back.

"Where the hell were you?" my father barks at me
as I round the corner. "I've been calling you.
Look. At. Her."

He says it with a desperate anger in his voice,
saliva shining on his lower lip.

I crouch on the floor next to him.
I have no idea what to do but
crumple at the sight.

And despite our hands on
her arms, her legs, her side,
there is nothing we can do to stop it.

Dad bends over her
Patrice Patrice Patrice
he keeps saying,
his voice thick with tears.

Then two huge men and
one brisk woman are there,
lifting her onto a stretcher,
checking her vitals.
She's stopped thrashing now,
but she's unconscious.

In this moment I feel I might lose her.
I'm frozen, can't move, can't speak.

Dad follows the paramedics into the ambulance.
"I'll call you from the hospital,"
he shouts at me
as the doors slam shut.
They zoom off into the dark.

Green Walls

At the hospital the next day
a brain surgeon — a real, live, actual
brain surgeon —
talks to us with sad eyes.
Mom's sleeping, white sheets over her thin body.
Sweat pools behind my knees from the
brown vinyl chair.

"You okay for her to hear this?"
the brain surgeon says,
angling his head in my direction.
"Yes," my dad says, taking my hand
for the first time since I was a tiny kid.

Stage four glioblastoma
Inoperable
Metastasized
Size of an orange
Not responding to treatment.

Dad looks at Mom.
Says nothing.
The doctor shifts in his chair,
wanting to stand.

"How much time?"
Dad says finally.

The doctor shrugs.
I'm sure he's shrugged like that
a thousand times,
delivering this sort of news.
"Weeks maybe," he says.
"We don't know how many."

"She'd want to be at home,"
my dad says.
"Not here."

"Of course,"
the brain surgeon says.
He touches my dad's shoulder and
then slips out without a sound.

Apocalypse

Because that's how it feels when
you hear the words
Stage four glioblastoma
associated with your mother.

Basically,
my mother's amazing, beautiful, wondrous brain
is eating itself to death.

I sit,
my own brain exploding in my skull.
Or maybe it's imploding.

I'm not sure.

Missives

You okay?

Sort of. Not really.

You were away sick today?

No. I'm not sick.

Want to meet at Bobby Sox in like an hour?
50s diner in town with greasy booths and
fried everything.

I look at my dad, sitting next to Mom,
holding her hand while she sleeps.

I feel useless,
I have no idea what I should be doing
except staring dumbly at the scuffed white floor.

"Merc," Dad says after a while. "Why don't you go
home and get some sleep. We've been up all night."

"No," I say, "I want to be with her."
I put my hand on Mom's skinny ankle.
It feels strange and foreign,
not like my mother at all.
Slowly, I return my hand to my lap.

"Go, Mercedes," my dad says. "She's
sleeping anyway. We're fine here."

I peel myself off the chair.
My legs are all kinked.
Once I'm outside the hospital,
breathing semi-fresh air again,
there's only one place I want to go.

And it's not Bobby Sox.

Safe Haven

First I text Ellis back.
Sorry. Can't today.

But if things weren't so life-alteringly
tragic right now, I think, *I would be all over it.*

M, are you okay?

I'll tell you later. Don't worry about me.

I mute my phone and toss it into my bag
as I reach the stoplights at Dewdney Trunk Road.
The semi-infrequent 701 bus is there, waiting,
as though I ordered it.

Five minutes away is the
brown 1970s house that's been my second home
since I was five.

At the front door I raise my hand to knock.
I pause.

I hope she's forgiven me by now.

Sandra's

My body is pure adrenaline,
sadness,
and exhaustion.

"Dude,"
she says, opening the screen door.
"Where were you today?"

"I know you're pissed at me,"
I say, "but I really
need you right now."

I tell her
all of it:
Ellis and I texting all night,
the seizure,
and the horrible, unthinkable diagnosis.

"Oh my god," Sandra says,
as she pulls me into a hug.
By now we're inside,
together in her living room.

We sit with that for a while.

Sandra's mom pauses in the doorway.
"You okay, sweetie?"
she says,
and that undoes me.
I sob.

She holds me like I'm a little child
on their velveteen chesterfield,
rocking me back and forth
for as long as I need.
Which is probably forever.

Home

My mother's friends start to
gather the next day.
Weavers, spinners, writers
painters, singers, midwives.

They beat red elk drums,
shake rattles, sing together,
circling my mother,
who's lying in bed and
smiling.

Patrice walks in beauty
Patrice walks in beauty

Mom has announced that she wants a
"death party"
rather than a funeral:
"Let it be while I'm still here.
I don't want to miss out on the fun."

They laugh, they cry.
They share stories.
They ask me to join them.

But I stand outside
my parents' bedroom.

I've known these women my whole life, but
I can't share my tears with them.

Stasis

If I look at her from just the right angle,
in just the right light,
she looks the same as ever.

Like now,
curled up in her favourite brocade chair,
long flaming hair intact,
silver rings on fingers,
reading Andy Warhol's diaries
for the thousandth time.

"Comfort read," she says,
holding it up.

I nod. "Want some tea?"

"I'm okay, hon."
She pauses, closes the book.
"Why don't you go out for a bit.
Don't feel you have to stay here
and be my nurse.
I've got Andy. I'm cool."

I stand there, unmoving.
I feel like I'm in the hospital again,
when Dad shooed me away.

"You're blocking my light," she says.
"Go. Hang out with Sandra.
Or you-know-who."
She looks up, head to one side,
mouth turned up at the corners.

Well

Now I have her blessing.

I don't even think about it.
My fingers are typing:

You still up for Snotty Box?

No reply.

An hour later:

OMG. Sorry. Snotty Box??

That's what we call it around here.

Ha ha. Sure, when?

45 minutes?

You're on.

I put my phone down,
hand shaking.

That was silly.
I'm still wearing my jeans and
Arcade Fire T-shirt from yesterday.
Or maybe it was even the day before that.

There's only one person to call at a time like this.

"I'm meeting Ellis at Bobby Sox
in, like, forty minutes,"
I say.

"You? Now? What?"
Sandra's voice sounds distant and echoey,
like she's in a big truck or something.

"Bobby Sox," I say. "Forty minutes."

"Dang," she says. "I'm out with Carl right now.
Driving to a show."

Oh. She *is* in a big truck.

"Sorry," she says. "I won't be there to help you.
But for whatever you wear,
whatever you say, just think, WWSD?"

"I think I'll manage," I say, laughing.

"And shave those man-hair legs of yours.
You never know what might happen."

Suburban Outfitters

The pink plastic razor slips from my shaking hand,
makes a bloody slice down the
front of my shin.

The thought of it,
the thought of possibly kissing
Ellis McShay,
made me do it.

Sandra knows;
she's the only one who knows
that he would be the first ever.

Shin patched up
(several large Band-Aids required),
I paw through my dresser drawer,
finally settle on polka-dot leggings,
black stretchy skirt, and my
Salvador Dali "melting clocks"
shirt. Might be a conversation starter,
who knows.

Mom's gone to bed
by the time I'm downstairs.
My dad consents to my
borrowing his old Mercedes,
the one I was allegedly conceived in
(thus, the namesake),
doesn't even ask what for.

Snotty Box

I get there first,
grab a booth in the back corner.
My forearms stick to the table.
No one I know is here tonight.
Thank goodness.

The one harried waiter is here,
with pleated pants and mullet.
He hates the high school students,
paying for our coffees in dimes and nickels,
using up all the creamers.

Five minutes later, or maybe seven
Ellis
comes toward me:
dark cuffed jeans, on the loose side,
black T-shirt, green army jacket.

He smells like
cookies and warmth and
all the good things in the world.

My eyes stare, unblinking.
I can't help myself.

"You look different than in math class,"
he says,
"or freezing outside an Odin's Sire show."

"Oh please," I say,
"let's leave them out of this."

Late Bloomer

I've never done this before.
Sixteen years old
and this is my first time ever
out with a guy.

The week has left me raw,
so raw I'm bristling with
confidence now.

Mercedes in charming, entertaining mode.
Not sure why,
but I'll take it.

We order fried pickles and milkshakes
(me, chocolate; him, strawberry).

"Let's play Quiz," he says.

"What's that? Some app?"

"No," he says.
"I hate small talk. Quiz lets us jump
right into the important stuff."

"Um, okay," I say. "You start."

Questions

Him: Favourite band or musician.

Me: Just one?

Him: Just one. That's why this is kinda hard.

Me: Fleetwood Mac.

Him: Really?

Me: For nostalgic purposes.

Him: And for non-nostalgic purposes?

Me: I thought we could only name one.

Him: I'll make an exception. Just this once.

Me: Björk. Because she brings art to music. You? Please not Odin's Sire.

Him: (laughs) St. Vincent.

Me: Nice. Favourite muppet?

Him: Ummm ... Grover.

Me: He's not a muppet. He's from *Sesame Street*.

Him: Technically, he is still a muppet. Okay, Miss Piggy.

Me: Interesting choice.

Him: Total babe. Favourite artist. Wait, Salvador Dali? [points to my shirt]

Me: Oh, that's cruel. You can't make me pick just one.

Him: But you have to.

Me: Favourite painter? Sculptor? Photographer? Installation artist? You'll have to narrow it down for me.

Him: Okay, fine. Painter.

Me: René Magritte.

Him: Phew. I'm glad it's not Dali. That would be clichéd.

Me: [Feeling my cheeks burn at choice of shirt] Whatever!

Him: Sorry. No judgment in Quiz.

Me: Your favourite painter?

Him: Norman Rockwell.

Me: For reals?

Him: For reals.

Me: He of the cheesy, white-bread Americana posters?

Him: Everything is alive in his pictures. Everything has character. Everything moves. That painting where the girl is showing her lost tooth to her friends? Each of their shoes is tied a different way. Genius.

Me: Jeez, and there you were making fun of me for Salvador Dali.

Him: Fair enough.

Me: My turn to ask. This tattoo. [Emboldened, I reach over to lift his sleeve with my pinky finger.] Meaning, please. I mean, a lily, really? [White with green stem.]

Him: [Pulls sleeve down.] I'll tell you another time. Favourite movie.

Something in his voice tells me not to press.

Me: *Groundhog Day.* You?

Him: *Die Hard.* But, *Groundhog Day*? The Bill Murray one? Why?

Me: It's all about self-actualization. It speaks to me.

Him: Define self-actualization.

Me: The realization or fulfilment of one's talents or potential.

Him: And are you in the process of self-actualizing?

Me: I don't know if it's something you can be aware of. Kind of like going crazy. If you think you are, you're probably not.

Him: Hmmmm. Interesting. So what does it mean to you to be self-actualized?

Me: To find my true artistic identity. And to be a world-famous artist. Like my mom.

10:00 p.m.

Crap.
I hadn't mentioned Mom
before this,
but it washes over me now.

I wanted to ask him about his
favourite food
favourite childhood memory
best elementary school teacher
most treasured possession
and now I won't be able to.

"You okay?"
Ellis says,
leaning across the booth,
eyes shiny with concern.

"I'm sorry," I say,
looking away.
"There are some things going on at home."

He deftly pays for our milkshakes
and says,
"It's okay."

This,
combined with those eyes of his,
unravels me.

Parking Lot

"Mercedes!"

It's the first time he's ever said my name.
He's shouting it after me
as I run out, scraping my wet face with my jacket cuff,
before he catches up to me in the parking lot.

"What's going on?"
He turns me to him,
holding both of my arms.

Months of lusting after his every move
and I can't believe I'm ruining it
with my stupid, stupid tears.
I don't know why I thought
I could hold it together.

Also:
Are sixteen-year-old boys usually this nice?

Nothing

I don't really want to talk about it right now.
I think I'll just go home.
I'm sorry. I'm sorry.
No, I'm fine. I can drive myself.
I'm sorry, I'm sorry.
I'm so sorry.

That Night

I pause outside my dad's closed door,
inspect my red, calloused, scratched-up hands.
Like Mom, I don't wear gloves:
we like to feel the material we're working with
on our skin.

I hear my dad flipping papers,
tapping on his old adding machine,
classic rock pumping out of his old clock radio.

I wonder how he'll do.
He has devoted his life to this.
I wonder what it'll be like after.
After.

I take a carton of Rocky Road ice cream from the freezer,
switch on *The Bachelor*,
pretend it's the jilted lovers I'm crying over.

Mess(ages)

Going to math class. See you there.

You're not here. WTF.

I wish you'd tell me what's up.

After a day of texts like these
he tried to call me.

I didn't pick up.
I was too busy outside

wiping the algae off the two-by-fours.

Proof

It seems a while ago now,
that day at the art gallery
when I was gripped with the fury
of proving myself.

That's what's been driving me,
pushing me ahead,
when all I'd rather do is watch movies
or stare out my window.

Seven weeks until the Wildwood application due date,
but I've got a more pressing timeline now.

Creation

Between the
death party
inside
and my father moping around
with sports and *Cheers* episodes
that he's not actually watching
24/7 on the TV,
the best place for me
this drizzling Saturday morning
is outside
with my ever-growing
beauty queen.

I haven't replied to Ellis's texts,
and I know that's a stupid move.

I'm like a carpenter out here now

wood nail hammer nail,
wood nail hammer nail.
The rhythm helps me forget.

Spotlight

That night
headlamp on
looking like a champ,
I hammer two-by-fours in the rain.
Legs are done,
hips are done,
backbone curves up slightly.
Now it's just arms, hands, head,
accessories.

Soon it'll be too tall
for me to reach the rest.

Behind me, I hear a creak.
I jump.
Dad's there
on an old patio chair.
Leaning slightly, one chair leg sinking into the mud,
right hand thrust into a bag of Hawkins Cheezies.

I say nothing.
The sound of nails still hammers in my head.
I'm a total mess.

"I've been on the phone
and email all day."
He proceeds to drop
the names of big art magazines.
"Word's getting out —
everyone wants last interviews."

Last interviews.
I hate it I hate it I hate it.
I want to throw my nails and hammer
and two-by-fours in the air.

"That's why I'm out here," I say.

Dad looks up again
through the rain and the dark.

"Tell me about her,"
he says,
pointing with his hand still in the Cheezies bag.

High

Dad rents me
a cherry-picker truck
to finish the rest,
rolls into the yard
with it the next morning.

I get to whirr up and down
in the little bucket
raising arms, head
wooden shoulders,
nailing it in from
ten feet in the air.

Hydraulics, man,
they're the best.

I pound in the
fingers, the thumbs,
with joints cleverly created
from twisted nails.
I'm getting much better
at hammering.

The beauty queen
rises up from the laurel bushes
in the corner of the yard.

I've almost got this.

Week After

Ms. Keyes waits at
the front steps
to catch me
on the way in to school.
She pulls me into her office.

"Mercedes."
She touches my arm.
"I've been thinking about you and your mom.
How is she?"
Tears start to gather
behind my eyes.

I shake my head because I'll cry if I answer.
After a moment, I say, "I've been working
on my Wildwood entry. It's almost done."

Ms. Keyes's face softens at that.
"Good," she says.
I start to explain my project to her but
I don't even have any photos on my phone.

My voice is normal at first,
but soon it devolves into
blubbering and unintelligible words.

Ms. Keyes brings me a cup of lemon tea,
rubs my back.

I should be embarrassed.
But I'm beyond that now.

She tells me to sit in her office
as long as I want
(which is good —
I didn't want to go
to math class anyway).

"I'd love to see the piece,"
she says,
then tiptoes outside
to teach a roomful of eighth graders
proper shading techniques.

P.R.

Mom's propped up in her favourite chair,
the green brocade one with the wood scrollwork,
old quilt on her lap,
her oddly blueish hands on top.

She's never sat in one place
for this long before.

All the women have gone for today.
It's just us,
the family three.
Mom choked down half a slice of
vegetarian pizza.
I managed one,
Dad ate the rest.

"Stop staring at me, you two,"
Mom says with a thin laugh.
"I don't want to live in a
funeral parlour."

A knock at the door,
and I think Dad and I
are both relieved to jump up.
I get there first.

It's a woman,
early thirties, maybe,
but I can never tell.

Dad rushes up behind me.
"She's not giving interviews,"
he says and starts to close the door.
I block it, painfully, with my right foot.

"Who are you?" I ask.
Dad grumbles behind me.

"Tana Schroeder," she says,
"*Vancouver Sun* arts reporter."
She flashes an important-looking
photo card, laminated on a string.

"I'm intrigued by this."
She gestures toward my beauty queen,
rising up beyond the lilac bushes and apple trees.
"Is this Ms. Stowell's final work?"
She says it matter-of-factly,
like she's not bothering us at all.

"It's mine," I say.
"I'm her daughter, Mercedes."

Without thinking,
barefoot and smiling,
I lead her into the yard.

Two Hours Later

A sharp rap at the door.

"Oh, for god's sake,"
my dad says, jumping up,
war face on.

Mom's gone to bed.
She usually makes it to
about 8:00 p.m. these days,
and he doesn't want her disturbed.

Dad flings the door open
ready to pounce
but this time it's just a
harmless-looking
teenaged boy.

Sheepish

"Sandra told me where you live."
He looks down,
the porch light making long shadows
of his feathery eyelashes.

Oh, Sandra,
I sigh inside my head.

I'm a mess.
My armpits stink,
my hair is greasy,
I'm kind of a wild woman.

But whatever.
He's here,
he came to me.

After quick introductions
and a scrutinizing up-and-down
look from Mr. Paul Stowell,
Ellis says to my dad:
"I love your house. This is amazing."

He's looking around,
his eyes flitting from
one cranny to the next.

"Why, thank you, son,"
my dad says
in his business voice.
"Designed it myself."

"Are you an architect?" Ellis asks.

"No, an art dealer. I got some help
with the blueprints from Sloane."
(Name-dropping, as usual.)

"Sloane Kim?" Ellis says, eyes wide.
He puts his hand on his chest,
perhaps in reverence.
"You know Sloane Kim?"

My dad's eyes widen too,
surprised that this young knickerbocker
knows about one of South Korea's
most prominent residential architects.

"I met her while doing some deals in Seoul,"
my dad says, and I fear this could turn
into a long night of stories.
It might, under normal circumstances.
But he tries to keep quiet now, in the evenings.
"I loved her work on the *Gimi* development."

Ellis is nodding away, excited.
"All those secret passageways
and tunnels," he says,
his voice raised a couple of octaves.
"Amazing."

I'm watching this exchange like a tennis match:
nerdy fanboy versus puffed-up middle-aged businessman.

"Yes, yes," my dad says in agreement.
He glances up the stairs to where
my mom's sleeping, then back to us.

"Anyway, something we can help
you with, young man?"
Ellis has some rumpled papers in his hand
that I hadn't noticed before.

"I was just bringing Mercedes
some math homework she missed,"
he says.

"That's very kind of you, Elton,"
my dad says. Ellis is too
polite to correct him.

"Yeah." I jump in. "Thanks, Ellis.
We can go over it in the living room."

Living, Room

Dad says goodnight and heads upstairs.
Ellis plops himself onto a chair,
the brocade one in the corner.
Mom's chair.

"No!" I say, my voice sharp,
before I can stop myself.
He leaps up.

"Sorry," I say. "But that one's, um, wobbly."

"Okay," he says, moving to the couch.
"I thought you were going to say
the ghost of Kurt Cobain
was sitting there or something."

A ghost. He has no idea,
the weight of his joke.

Bathroom

"I'll be right back.
Feel free to look at the books
or whatever."

I close the bathroom door,
still not believing that
Ellis McShay is on the
other side of it.
It's so wrong.
He shouldn't be here.
I should ask him to leave.
But there's something I need to ask him.

Pieces

When I emerge, less than two minutes later
(worrying he might disappear,
possibly, if I took too long)
Ellis is flipping through
my portfolio,
prepped and ready to go for
my application.

"How do you know who Sloane Kim is?"
I say. "No one knows about Sloane Kim."

"There's something you should
know about me," he says.
"When I'm into something, I'm *really* into it.
Deconstructivist architecture. Basically obsessed."

How is it that the goddesses
(or whoever is in charge)
sent me this gorgeous, fascinating
specimen of a boy
at the exact wrong time in my life?

My heart's bumping and
I wonder where I should sit.
Sandra says I overthink things.
I settle on about a foot away
on the couch.

"I came over to make sure you're okay,"
he says.

"I'm okay," I lie.

"You can come closer, you know."
He pats the cushion next to him,
looking up
with those eyes
that take a little piece of me
every time.

Electrical Work

He flicks through the
black pages —
photos of *Quality Time*,
me holding awards,
sketches of the beauty queen.
My whole artistic brain spilled out.

"Wow, so you're kind of an
amazing artist."

I feel his warmth
like a
zap.

"*Please* don't mention that drawing of you."

"Well," he says, in mock horror.
"I was trying not to bring it up, but there you go."
He laughs. I giggle, my cheeks hot.

Then he lifts the book
to inspect more closely,
so focused.

Meanwhile I'm
inspecting him.

He asks more questions
about my portfolio.
Seems genuinely interested.

I tell him about
Wildwood and the
crazy deadline.
Telling him this
is so much easier than
telling him about
Mom.

Already Knew

He says he has a confession.

"I already knew you were an artist."

"Huh?"

"Google."

"Oh, god."

"That dollhouse you made
when you were ten was pretty creepy.
In a cool way."

"Thanks, Ontario Provincial
Karate Champion."

His cheeks go red
through the freckles.

We go back to the portfolio,
his long fingers turning the pages
slowly, carefully.

"So you wouldn't be here
next year
if you get into this school."

We lift our heads at the same time.
The eye contact almost makes me
black out.

I explain that
I'd just be in Vancouver,
and could come home
on weekends.

"That's *so* not the
same thing as having you
at school."

"Who are you? Sandra?"
I say, picking hard at some
threads on the couch cushion.
"She's always banging on
about that."

It's true, though:
the thought of not being with them
makes my chest freeze,
stabbed by a large icicle.

I Guess I'll Have To

Make the most of you
while you're still here.

His words exactly.

Yards and Yards

My legs are twitching like crazy.
Nervous energy. Adrenal glands on overload.
I jump up.

"Let's get out of here.
Go for a walk or something."

He sets my portfolio aside. "Okay."

Moments later,
we're out in the April chill.
Ellis surveys the yard,
spots the huge wooden woman
looming above the fruit trees.
"So that's your art school entry, then."

"Yeah."

"Why didn't you mention it?
If I'd made that
I'd be pretty stoked about it."

I pause.
It's true,
I didn't feel compelled
to show it to him,
like I did to the newspaper reporter,
hungry for exposure.

"I dunno," I say.
"It's so late. Don't your parents care
where you are?"

"No. But you're changing
the subject."

Like, Like

"Why do you like me?"
I imagine Sandra shuddering
if she knew I said that.
"After, uh, you know …
it became clear that
I'm an obsessive fangirl?"

His head tips back,
he laughs.
God, I love his laugh.

In my limited experience,
boys my age don't laugh so easily
so spontaneously
so kindly.

"That was when I knew that you liked me, for real."

I feel my mouth twist up at the edges,
dubious.

"You're this super cute girl,
with cat head dresses
[he noticed!]
and photos of driftwood sculptures
on your binder.
I didn't know what to say to you
before that."
His shoulders go up,
then down.

"I designed that cat head fabric
myself," I say (I can't help it).
"There's this website
called Spoonflower where you can
make your own prints."

"See," he says, "what did I say?
So cool."

"What about Brittany Winters?"
I say it. I can't help myself.

He clucks his tongue.
"Well, she's just not very nice,
is she?"

"I'm glad you realized that."

Before I can say anything else,
he's kissing me.

It's warm
and delicious,
probably like the first time
I ever ate a cookie,
but a thousand times better.
His lips are soft,
his breath hot.
I sigh.
I want to fall into him,
but
for some reason

memories of that
day at Bobby Sox
flood me.

I think about Mom now,
sick.
So sick.

And I'm out here
with Ellis.

I shouldn't be having fun
at a time like this.

Salt

I'm crying.

"What?" Ellis says,
pulling away from our kiss.
He licks my tear away
from the corner of his mouth.

All I can think of is
Mom,
her brain betraying her.

"I'm sorry," I say.

Then the words gush, and
I can't stop them.

"My mom,
she's sick.
Really sick."

"What do you mean,
sick?"

"Like,
going to die
sick."
I choke out
the words, my voice thick with more tears.

"Where is she? The hospital?"

"Here. Upstairs."

He looks away.
His eyes
are different.
Distant.

"Shit,"
he says.

Now he's the one
apologizing,
stumbling away from me.

"Oh my god. I'm sorry.
I feel like such an ass."

"No," I say. "You didn't know."

He looks toward my house,
flinches, just enough for me to notice.

"Mercedes, please don't think I'm a jerk,
but I—I have to go."

He's in his car in five seconds,
leaving me with his taste on my lips,
wondering what the hell.

Inside, I sit on the floor next
to Mom's chair,
lay my head on the brocade.

It smells like her:
cloves and steel and leather.

Dawn

I wake as the light flicks through
the living room window.
I'm still on the chair,
my neck at a ridiculous angle.

Mom's there, on the couch, tea in hand.
I wonder how long she's been watching me.
Her eyes are shiny.

I raise my head. *Ow.*

"You used to fall asleep like that
when you were a little girl," she says.
"Dad or I had to carry you off to bed."
She laughs, her voice soft.
"Sorry I missed Ellis last night.
Or Elliot, as your dad said."

"Last night he was calling him Elton."

My mom laughs again. "He's hopeless."

"They bonded over architects," I say.
"Bit of a bromance going on now,
I think."

"He sounds like a catch, Mercedes."
She pats my shoulder.
I *thought* he was.

Free Period

"What an ass."

That's Sandra's summation of the
current situation the next day at school.
She leans against the lockers with
a metallic *thwack*, her binder clutched to
her chest in thought.

"I can't believe he just left,"
she says. "Who just leaves a cute,
sobbing girl like that?"
She pauses. "You know, though,
sickness *is* hard for some people to handle."

That's why I love Sandra. She'll completely
analyze a scenario with barely any
participation from me.

It's our free period,
before I have history, and she has P.E.

We wander to the cafeteria
talking low
because he could be around any corner.

But, as it turns out,
I don't see him all day.

In Transit

I usually walk
but today I take the bus home.

I'm tired lately.
Tired of getting through the days,
the relentlessness of it all.
And now,
what is up with Ellis?

I take a novel out of my backpack
White Teeth, by Zadie Smith,
because it's set in London and I've
always dreamed of going there.
But I can't focus.

It's like
I'm here
but not here.

Myself
but not myself.

Symbols

The house is filled
with the pungency of
patchouli and B.O. and vanilla.
I retreat to my bedroom.

It's been another day
of women here
dancing, singing, cooking —
they took roses and hydrangeas
and blossoms from the yard
to make a huge mandala,
radiating out from a
heart of rose petals,
forming a circle around it.
I can see it from my bedroom window.

I feel the pull of the mandala,
at once geometric and organic,
and it's like I can smell the papery sweetness
of the rose petals from up here.

I feel the pull of these
warm, earthy women
I've grown up with,
and now I want to join them.

I go out into the yard,
pick up some leaves and
scatter them around
the edges of the mandala.
My little contribution.

Then
the women form a circle,
holding hands.

I don't usually do this sort of thing.
Today I want to.

My mother is across the circle
and she walks, dignified,
to stand next to me,
holding my hand.

Hers is thin and shaky
but here she is,
still next to me.

Then Dad's there too —
usually he'd bellow something like
"What's this hen party all about?"
Today he's quiet,
grasping mom's other hand,
gentle.

My family.

We walk slowly
around and around,
humming softly.

Alouette

Mom's down at the river
the next morning before school.
I bring coffees and sit with her
(mainly in silence)
because she's communing with
the spirit of the river.

"I hope it gets warm enough,"
she says,
"for me to swim here one last time."

It's not like her to be so dramatic.

More silence.

Then:
"Do you remember the story I used to tell you?"

"Of course,
of course I do," I say.
"It's part of my childhood mythology."

Saturday

All that's left to do
for Miss Haney
is her bouquet,
to be laid across her
long thin arms.

Rebar.
And there's only one
room in this house
that would have it.

I figure there's
no way Mom will be in there.
It's already past
eight o'clock.

"Mercedes!"
She smiles,
sweeps something
into a drawer.

"What are you doing in here?"
I say.

She looks around.
"Um, in my studio?"

"Yeah, I didn't think ..."

"I wasn't tired. I felt
like poking around a bit."

She finds the rebar for me,
but she's too weak to lift it.
My formerly strong,
metal-bending mother,
reduced to this.

"What's it for?" she asks.
Her cheeks are sunken,
but her eyes still have sparks.

I bind five pieces of the heavy wire
with two zip ties.

"Her bouquet. To lay across her arms."

Mom nods. "Nice."

"I'm going to show her to you soon, Mom.
Real soon. Don't look yet."

Mom smiles,
reaches over,
strokes my hair
like she did when I was little.
When she told me the story of the
river mermaid,
the beautiful woman with
the shimmering trout tail
who lived in the Alouette.

I ask her to tell it to me
now.

Bits and Pieces

When ocean mermaids die
they turn to sea foam,
green bubbles that lap the shore.

When river mermaids die
they turn to pine needles,
bits of branches and bark,
tiny stones and leaves
that float downstream.

I remember when I was little,
arranging screws and rivets in buckets at her feet,
her smoker's voice above me,
steel wool whisking across
a vintage bed frame, or a winding length of old pipe
rubbed in circles to reveal the beauty of the metal.

She would tell me
the story of the river mermaid
who once lived in the Alouette River.

The river mermaid with the rainbow trout tail,
with sparkles in her hair,
who died from the pain of love.

I never understood, though.
I never understood
what she meant by that.

Later, In the Darkness

I throw on my boots
and climb the ladder,
rebar and tin roses bouquet
slung against my back
like a quiver of arrows.

It's raining, and the rungs are slippery.
I really should have someone here to help me,
but I'm determined.

Don't look down, don't look down.

Trembling, I reach Miss Haney's arms,
heave the bouquet across them.
The finishing touch.

Then I descend, quick as I can,
hop off the ladder with a splash in the mud below.

I look up. She's done.
She's *done*. It's all there.

But there's no ta-da moment.

I look around, as though I'll find my excitement
around here somewhere.
Maybe it's just hiding.

Crit

Ms. Keyes frowns when
I show her the photos,
squinting at the details.

She takes my phone,
zooms in and out
taking in
the hair
    (ringlets of thin-planed pine)
the orange construction-mesh skirt
    (taken from a vacant lot)
the bouquet
    (a little heavy, but it'll hold)
the two-by-four arms and legs
    (the terrible nailing isn't too visible)

"She's amazing, Mercedes." She pauses.
"Are you happy with it?"

Sometimes I hate Ms. Keyes's questions.
On the surface, Miss Haney does look amazing.

But Ms. Keyes knows there's no life to her.
And she knows that I know that too.

"Of course I'm happy with it,"
I say, like the sometimes-petulant
teenager that I am.

Plans

I'm going to make my mom
breakfast in bed tomorrow,
I decide,
then do the big reveal.

She's an imposing sight,
that Miss Haney,
rising up from her wooden platform,
almost eleven feet tall.

I wonder if she'll be

enough.

Front Page

LOCAL TEEN ARTIST GOES BIG

Maple Ridge artist Mercedes Stowell has big dreams. Her latest piece, an eleven-foot-tall recycled materials sculpture she's dubbed *Miss Haney*, is set to make a larger-than-life social statement — and, she hopes, it will serve another purpose as well. Stowell plans to use the sculpture as her entry to the prestigious Wildwood Fine Arts School, a private Vancouver institution that birthed the careers of many well-known artists, including her mother, world-renowned sculptor Patrice Stowell.

"It's a commentary on societal attitudes toward beauty," the well-spoken Stowell says. "This beauty queen is constructed from old boards and nails, just as so-called beauty is constructed from fake nails, makeup and airbrushing."

Last year Stowell's found-materials piece *Quality Time*, which featured more than 200 My Little Ponies attached to a vintage couch, was created with a Wildwood Fine Arts School application in mind. Although that piece did not successfully gain her entry, she's pulled herself back up and decided to go even larger scale. The community's fingers are crossed for this young talent.

— Tana Schroeder, reporter, *Vancouver Sun*

I didn't mention
Quality Time to her.
But of course she found out
somehow.

Back Page

Patrice Magritte Stowell
April 26, 1970 – April 26, 2019

It is with great sadness that we announce the passing of
Patrice Stowell after a brief yet courageous battle with
cancer. Patrice leaves to mourn her beloved daughter
Mercedes, devoted husband Paul, sister Marie and many
friends, colleagues and fans. Predeceased by her parents,
Phyllis and Lloyd Baker, of Kaslo, BC. A leader in the modern
art world, Patrice was a talented sculptor and metal artist.
No service by request. In lieu of flowers, donations to the
Wildwood Fine Arts School Scholarship Fund are gratefully
accepted.

Cake

Yesterday was my mother's
forty-ninth birthday, her fiftieth year on this earth.

Still beautiful
her hair wild and white and orange
like the flames of a campfire,
spread out over her pillow.

That morning in the kitchen
my dad was whipping up
cream cheese icing for a
carrot cake.
Mom's favourite.

"You know she won't be able to eat that,"
I said.

"Maybe a nibble," he said.
Together we placed three candles
right in the centre,
our little family.

I carried the cake, singing.
Dad led the way to the bedroom
and stopped.

I blew out the candles.

The light had gone out.

Inundated

My father's phone is
constantly ringing.
His emails are
constantly dinging.
He's already put a
message on her website
with the news.

His office door open,
I hear him say,
"Yup, yup, we're just
moving forward, moving forward,"
about two dozen times a day

as though we're a breaker
pushing through
islands of ice in the ocean.

House of Pain

Forget anything I ever said before
about stiletto-heel kicks to my chest.

I didn't know what pain was
until now.

It overcomes me,
this tsunami of grief.
My hands gripping
the edge of the sheet
when I wake up.

I pound the mattress with my fist.

I sob so hard
it's silent.

BFF

Everyone's texting me about the front page,
but some haven't read further in.

I told Sandra the news
right away,
of course.

OMG. Can I bring you anything?

Yes. I'd like my mom back, please.

She brings me a frappuccino
(I drink half)
and we sit in silence for two hours,
my head on her shoulder,
not crying,
but not talking either.
Ten years of friendship
between us.

Sitting

I've taken to sitting
in three places.

One: under the beauty queen,
between her legs,
looking up like she's
some bizarre, crooked, wooden
Eiffel Tower.

Two: on the roof,
rubbing my palms
along the rough shingles.
Enjoying the pain,
wanting the pain.

Three: on the family rock,
to torture myself
because my heart feels
like it's being ripped
into shredded pieces
when I'm there.

I Don't Like To

Go into the house
walk past her studio
walk past their bedroom,
because it's like she just stepped out
to buy some wine and paper towels
and she'll come through the
front door any minute,
complaining about traffic.

Maybe if I'd noticed the headaches sooner.
Maybe if I'd tried to make her rest more.
Maybe if I got her to quit smoking sooner.
Maybe if I told Dad to stop making her work so hard.

She'd still be here,
bustling in through the front door,
silver necklaces clicking together,
laughing her raspy laugh.

Revolving

It pissed me off that her art came first.
If I have kids, I'll always go to their school concerts,
remember their parent-teacher conferences,
pack their lunches, tell them I love them.
Be there.

It was like Patrice Stowell
belonged to the world.

And now,
my mom isn't here at all.
Before there was at least
the reassurance
of her physical being,
her vitality, her sparkle.

Where does that *go* when people die?

I don't understand,
not even with one morsel of my being

how that can just disappear.

Midnight

I'm between
Miss Haney's legs again.
Trying to distract myself.

All I have to do is
take some photos and
write my artist's statement,
but my brain is
jammed
like a transmission that
can't change gears.

What was I thinking?
Have I ever even
cared for a second
about society's attitudes
toward beauty?

This thing just ticks all the boxes.

They didn't like a couch covered in ponies.

I thought I should give them what they want.

Sometimes You Kick

I stomp around Miss Haney,
looking at her from all angles.

I want to kick her
all of a sudden.
So I do.

I rage and grunt and flail
and kick the crap out of
the high heels
the legs
anything I can get at.

Miss Haney has absolutely
no moxie.

She has no heart.

She's a huge flaming
pile of shit.

12:16 a.m.

You awake, E?

12:20 a.m.

I know you're not talking to me right now.

I don't know why.

12:24 a.m.

But I need you.

12:31 a.m.

Because I'm about
to do something stupid.

In Medias Res

I sent him that text
to spring me into action.

I've already
splashed the gas,

lit the match.

I feel like I'm watching from above
out of my body
staring but not feeling.

It's truly a brilliant spectacle of
towering, blazing orange
flickering around the wooden body,
burning her at the stake.

I watch
I just did that, I really did that
for five minutes, maybe ten.

"What the hell?"
It's Dad,
running out in his boxers,
big belly jiggling,
surprised
to see an eleven-foot-high
wooden likeness of a woman
engulfed in flames.

He's shouting.
I'm numb.
He grabs the garden hose.
The tiny stream piddles on the fire.
The flames burn higher.

He runs into the house
and I stand there.

Frozen.

Red and White and Orange

I don't know what the big deal is.
The fire is nowhere near the house.

A small crowd of neighbours has gathered
in their pajamas and slippers,
the flames like a sun in
the corner of our yard.

The firefighters
jump out of their truck,
the look of duty on their faces.

Strong hands grab
my shoulders from behind me,
pulling me back.

Ellis.

He doesn't speak
just spins me around
orange flickering in his eyes.

Reasons

After
the firefighters packed up their gear

after
my dad said he'll speak to me in the morning

after
everyone has left, back to their beds

Ellis and I sit on the porch steps,
Miss Haney scorched and crumbling
before us.

It's 1:00 a.m. or something, and
he's just returned with small
cups of 7-Eleven coffee
French vanilla with whitener.

"This is the second time you've
brought me a hot beverage in Styrofoam," I say.

He looks at me, quizzical.

"Odin's Sire," I say.

He slaps his hand to his forehead.
"The regret I felt after not
giving you my hoodie.
What an idiot."

"Sandra and I called you
an enigma after that."

"That's me." He draws himself up,
fake-puffs his chest out.

I sip.
Ponder my life.

"I know that anger,"
he says after his own sips.
"I know why you did it."

I look over at him. "You do?"

"I smashed dishes.
I kicked in headlights.
I ripped apart pillows."

It takes me a few minutes
but then it all comes together.

"Lily," I say,
thinking about that
flower on his shoulder,
white with a green stem.
I feel foolish for
not figuring it out sooner.

He nods,
then sucks in a quick breath.
"Mom."

"Why didn't you tell me?" I say.

"It's still hard to talk about," he says.
"It's been more than a year,
and it still kicks my guts out
on a regular basis."

I want to ask more, but I hold back.

"It was ALS," he says. "It started with a
twinge in her back, then weak legs.
A year and a half later she was in bed.
She couldn't move anything except her eyes.
My dad took care of her non-stop."

"Oh my god."

"Sorry," he says. "You don't need
to hear this right now."

I touch my foot to his foot. "But I do."

He tells me they moved from Toronto after that,
here to Maple Ridge,
where his uncle and father now co-own
a karate dojo.
"We just had to escape," he says.
"My dad and I never talk about her now."

I nod. "My dad and I haven't
talked about it either."

Ellis steps toward me, hugs me.
The sky is becoming lighter.
We stay there a while.

It's a warm, still, sighing sort of hug,
an embrace between two people
who know the same wrench of grief.

Rubble

Everyone wants to know why.
Why I did it,
why I ruined my chance.
My dad shakes his head at me —
before I was a disappointment,
but now I'm plain crazy.

Sandra seems pleased,
in her way,
because this might mean
I'll stay put.

Ellis, though,
Ellis understands.

Groundswell

"It's like it comes in waves," he says,
"and you never know when
the next one will hit."

We're in his dad's Subaru,
and he's talking to me about sadness.

He texted me after school
(I didn't go, of course,
not yet)
to see if I needed to escape
the house for a while.

My aunt is at my house now,
cooking for us and making tea.
I love her,
but the weight of memories inside,
bits of my mother everywhere,
it's too much to be around.

"Does it fade?" I say. "You know,
when you wake up in the morning,
and it feels so wrong that the world
is going on as normal,
and you want to scream?"

"It fades," he says,
shifting as he turns a corner.
"But then you feel guilty for not
feeling that way quite as much
anymore."

I watch his long, capable fingers
on the gearshift,
pushing up, pulling down.

The wanting of him is still there
(I'm aware of it in
a distant sort of way),
but the lust is on hold,
for now.

"Do you have any photos of her?" I say
when we're parked on the beach at Whonnock Lake.

There's no one else here
on a rainy Tuesday afternoon.
We've described our childhoods
(parts of them, anyway)
and our memories,
opening up all those
little pieces of ourselves.

He takes his phone out of his pocket,
pauses a moment.

"It's okay," I say. "You don't have to show me."

He passes his phone to me.
"You can Google her.
Lily McShay."

"I don't have to."

"I want you to."

Her photo stares out at me
from the Google Images search.
Brown hair, shoulder length,
freckles like Ellis,
closed-mouth smile, lab coat.
Beautiful.

"She was a family doctor,"
he says. "She taught at the
University of Toronto. Knew
what was wrong
before she even got
the official diagnosis."

He sniffs, wipes his eyes
with the back of his hand.
"Sorry. I haven't talked
about this in a while."

We sit in silence, watching
the spring wind
ripple tiny waves on the lake.

Fame

"She's like a rock star or something,"
he says, tilting his phone away
from the late-afternoon glare.
He's looking at my mom's iconic photo,
the one from *Sculptors of the Modern Era*.
She's laughing at the camera,
ring-clad hand casually touching her cheek,
the headshot she used for just about everything.

"She was sort of a rock star. A rock star
of the modern sculpture world."

He puts down his phone. "Wow."

"Are we doing this to torture
ourselves?" I say.
"Looking at these photos,
talking like this?"

He looks out at the lake again,
eyes narrowed.
Slowly, he shakes his head.

"No. This is good."
He takes my hand,
squeezes.

Four Days Later

Saturday, Sandra and I have an all-day
John Hughes Marathon:

Ferris Bueller's Day Off
Pretty in Pink
Some Kind of Wonderful

I don't feel like going home after.

I text Ellis:

Can I come over?

Now?

Yeah.

22484 Stuart Crescent
Buzzer 401

Why I'm Here

I'm not sure, exactly,
why I'm standing in Ellis's
laminate-floored entranceway,
but I'm happy to be here.

He and his father live in an apartment
in a new-ish building
off the main street in town.
In the living room is just a brown sectional
and a wall-mounted TV,
a mixed martial arts bout on pause and
a half-eaten pepperoni pizza
on the coffee table.

"Looks like I'm interrupting quite the night,"
I say.

"My dad's not home," he says.
(I hadn't even thought of that.)
"Want some?" he nods toward the pizza.
I shake my head.

He turns off the TV, shuffles his feet.
"Um, can I get you a Coke or something?"

He seems like he's not sure
what to do with me now that I'm standing
here in his house.
His unexpected vulnerability
warms the aching parts of me.

I should be nervous,
but I'm not.
I whisk off my scarf and jacket,
drape them on the back of the couch.

I know exactly what I'm going to do
when Ellis returns from the kitchen.

After all the days of grief,
the knots and the clenched stomach
and the crying,
I want to be cleansed.

I Feel Like

I've never felt so, so
unbridled.

At my kiss, he says,
"Really?"

"Really."

I kiss him again,
harder this time.
His breath shudders
as his lips brush mine.

He throws the cans of Coke
onto the couch,
picks me up like I weigh
two pounds (not the case),
lowers me onto the floor,
a fleece blanket smoothed under me.

Shirts Off

His breath blazes on my skin.
He's all pale skin and freckles
and firmness.

"You're so beautiful,"
he says, over and over.
I feel the same way,
of course,
except that I cannot speak.

The kissing is my favourite part
(understatement).
I brush my lower lip
against his top lip
my back to the floor.

His fingers comb through my hair
follow the line of my eyebrows
my eyelids
my lips.
His long bangs brush my forehead.

In the dim light I see
the perfect mole on his right cheek
and circle it with my index finger.

We spend a while like this,
tracing parts of each other.

Fifteen minutes, half an hour, who knows.

Exhale

I'm on top
I have no idea
what I'm doing
but somehow it seems
to be coming
naturally.

Soft Landing

We lie together,
a jumble of legs and arms,
and I wonder if I'm supposed
to feel like a changed woman
or something.

After That

The family rock
is the only place that calls me —
sometimes with Ellis,
sometimes with Sandra,
sometimes alone.

I spend two whole days there,
watching the river bubble past.

Nothing's changed in its world.

Hands

Dad shows up at the rock.
He's brought McDonald's.

As he plows into his Big Mac,
mouth full:
"So, how you doing, Merc?"

As though it's just some
regular day. I shrug.

You worked Mom too hard,
I want to say to him.
Take him by his shoulders and shake him.
You always wanted more money,
more more more.
Maybe if you hadn't,
she would have lived.

But I don't say any of that.
Perhaps someday I will.

"Here," my dad says. "Close your eyes."

I play along.

"Okay."

(I hear him wiping
his hands on his jeans)

"Pick a hand."

I open my eyes.
Dad's looking at me,
expectant.

"That one." I point.
I'm suddenly five years old again.

He brings out an empty hand. "Nope."

I sigh. "That one."

He opens his thick palm.

I gasp.

It's a heart,
full and textured
made of thin metal strips

intertwined.

Inside, a smaller heart dangles.

I remember Mom sweeping something
into a drawer
when I asked her to
tell me the story.

I take it,
turn it over in my hand.
Hold it to my own heart.

Patrice Stowell's last piece.
She made it for me.

Truth & Beauty

Dad goes back into the house,
but I stay by the river.

I could watch it for hours,
the water rippling along.

The rock feels imbued with the soul
of her,
of Mom.

It's like she imprinted the rock
with her very presence
from so many years of sitting here.

She wanted me to pursue my art,
devote my time to it,
live it, breathe it.

That's what I want to do.
That's what I need to do.

I hold up my new metal heart,
ready to follow where it leads me.

Pieces

Ocean mermaids become sea foam
when they die;
river mermaids become bits of
moss, twigs, needles and bark.

I hear Mom's smoky voice
whispering this in my ear.

I snap a dry branch into pieces,
fling the splinters into the river.
Then some mulch, then pine needles.

They flow downstream,
out of sight.

My head has been in
a polluted haze,

but now
I jump up,
scrabble through
vines and branches,
scrape up a pile of fallen needles,
moss, bark, twigs, tiny branches,
other forest floor things.

Perfect.

By noon
on the family rock
curving along its edge,
pieces laid out in waving lines,
moss sprinkled on,
and leaves.
I've shaped the outline of a tail.

Look

I bring Dad outside,
stand beside him,
gesturing with a flourish.

His eyes follow
the swoop of the tail,
down to the river.

"Jesus."
He wipes his face with his hand.
"I almost forgot that story."

He's quiet then,
for a while.

We both look out,
and it's like she could be there
in her long green skirt,
wading into the cool water
like she belonged to it.

More

More sticks
more branches
more moss
more twigs

As I gather them
I look down at my hands
and smile.

My fingers are
fast becoming talons
like my mother's.

My phone buzzes in my
back jeans pocket,
just as a vision solidifies
in my brain.

Him: **Feel like going to Snotty Box?**

Me: **Can't right now.**

I snap a quick photo of my growing pile,
send it with my text.

What is it?

I'll tell you later. But can you do me a favour?

Bring you a chocolate peanut butter milkshake? Sure.

Ha ha. Go to the hardware store and
get me the best construction glue they have.

Just the glue, then?

And the milkshake.

I stop. Realize my briskness.
Sorry. Thank you.

Ellis sends back the kissy face emoji.
He knows I hate emojis.
I smile and
get back to work.

Four Days Later

It's a meditation.
With each twig
is a memory.
With each branch
is an emotion.
I move through it all:
anger, guilt, love, happiness,
wondering when I'll reach
acceptance.

Swooping lines of bark and twigs
form a tail,
almost dipping into the river.

Leaves and branches
curve into a torso,
a head and arms.

Even as I build it
the river laps up and
washes it away,

pine needles, bits of twig
and bark,
floating downstream.

Small sticks encircle the metal heart
on the left side of her chest,
affixed to the rock

with Liquid Nail's Fuze It All-Surface Construction
Adhesive.
(Ellis really came through.)

When everything else is washed away,
the heart will remain.

Done

On the sixth day
I create her hair.
Wild grasses and morning glory vines,
birch bark and long strands of moss
flutter out from her head of twigs.

After that I adjust and readjust,
putter and fuss over her for a time,
until finally I stand back.

I take in the full length of her,
poised gracefully on the family rock.

She's done.

She's *done*.

I don't need to search around
for my excitement this time.
I feel a squeal of thrilled-ness
brewing in my chest.

The sparkles of exhausted satisfaction
bubble up and burst out of me
like a cork out of a champagne bottle.

Major ta-da moment.

She Would

On the seventh day
I make my big reveal.

"Your mom would be so proud,"
Sandra says, her eyes following
the curve of the mermaid's tail.

Ellis nods, pulls me in to him.
"It's incredible, Mercedes."

I invited them here to
show them why
I've basically been ignoring them for days.

My mom *would* be so proud.
I know she would.

I'm proud of myself.
The wire heart is my heart,
spilled out for all to see.

This makes
my body brim over,

as though my insides
are swelling
with tears and heartache
and bittersweet.

When the tears do come,
they are a different chemistry
than those that preceded them
for all those days.

They're streaming, cool,
healing tears.
Like the river.

The river that was more
a part of my mother,
almost,
than her own blood.

We all admire the river mermaid
for a while longer, walking around her,
Ellis and Sandra making appreciative
comments about details
like the shiny pebbles
strewn over her tail,
and the golden flecks of
pyrite in her eyes.

Then Ellis leaves to teach a karate class,
and it's just me and Sandra.

"Dude." She turns to look at me.
"You're using this for
your application, right?"

"It's not about
the Wildwood application anymore.
It's for her," I say.

"Why can't it be both?
You're not going to
let it wash away — and that's that."

I kick at the rocky ground.
"Making it was doing
something with it. It was
about the process. Besides,
I wouldn't feel right using it."

"Listen to me," Sandra says. She takes me by the shoulders.
"This is amazing. It's so *you*.
It totally honours your mom.
Using it for the application won't take away from that."

"No."

"Yes. Imagine if your mom were here right now.
She'd want you to use this for your application."

"How do you know?" I say.

Sandra rakes her hands through her hair.
"You're exasperating."

"What's the point, though?
It's due tomorrow. Forget it."

My face is screwed up,
my cheeks pressing up into my eyeballs,
and I can't set it to rights.

I pace,
fling myself around,
monologue to Sandra
about how
there's no time,
about how
maybe I don't even want to go
there anyway.

About how

maybe I don't even care anymore.

Sandra looks straight into my eyes.

"Yes, you do.
You're effing entering this."

"Why are you saying this?
You don't even want me to go."

"Can you blame me?
You're my best friend. I want us to go
to prom together, be in classes together,
graduate together. There's nothing wrong
with wanting that."

"You've never even cared about my art," I snarl.

"What makes you think I don't care about your art?"
Sandra snarls back. "You've been obsessed with it
the whole time I've known you."

"Yeah, and you've made fun of me the whole time."

"In a loving way!" Sandra counters.

"In a selfish way," I say.
"I tried to be normal for you.
I tried to be normal and not give a shit."

"You think I don't give a shit?" she says.
"I give a shit about our friendship.
You only give a shit about your art."

I turn away, back to the mermaid.

"Fine," Sandra says. "If that's how you want it.
I'll go."

An Hour Goes By And

I'm still staring at the mermaid.
My vision is blurring.
I keep forgetting to blink.

My mom cared about art more than anything.
Even me, sometimes.

Sandra's words shatter in my ears.
Am I the same?

I'm numb, though.
I'm tired and I can't think anymore.

Moments later,
I hear heavy boots clomp up behind me.

"Good," Sandra says. "You're still here."

I say nothing. I don't turn around.
So numb.

"Mercedes,
I know you're meant to go to Wildwood."

I open my mouth
without knowing what I'm about to say.
Sandra places her finger over my mouth.
"Shush."

I shush.

"Of course I'll miss you," she says.
"But consider this your *Good Will Hunting* moment.
You know? When Ben Affleck tells Matt Damon
he hopes that one day when he goes to pick him
up in the morning to go to their menial jobs,
he won't be there. Because he was destined for
something greater."

Something bigger.

Tick Tock Tick Tock

"Okay,"
I say finally.
"Let's *do* this."

Sandra runs home for her
camera (a fancy one).
I write an artist's statement.
Sandra formats it with nice fonts
(she's good at that stuff).
We print it all,
put it in a bubble envelope.

We send off the package
five minutes before the
FedEx office closes.

May, End of

Waiting.
Waiting.

On Hold

This summer is at a standstill.
Hazy days bleed into
humid nights.
Sandra and I pass the days
curtains closed
watching movie after movie
like we always do.

"Sandra," I say to her,
in the middle of *Dirty Dancing*
one afternoon:

"I want you to know
that I think about it —
what it will mean
if I do get into Wildwood."

Sandra pauses the movie,
sits up, looks at me sideways.

"No more laughs at our lockers,"
I continue.
"Lunch together in the back bleachers.
Creative Writing class together.
Walking home.
Of course I think about it."

"Really?"
Sandra says, dubious.

"It's true, believe me,"
I say. "I mean, obviously.
It's like sharp pointy things,
poking at my heart."

"You nerd," she says.

But then she sits next
to me on the sectional,
gives me her last handful
of Smarties,
presses play on the movie
and we sing along:

I've had the time of my life.

Canadian Tuxedo

The next morning
I head down to the rock.

I want to see how my girl is doing.
As the river rises,
the water has lapped up and swept
away the sticks and leaves and branches
nearest to the edge, just as I'd imagined.

I move some loose moss, and
line up some sticks along the edge,
tinkering with it a little.

I look up.
There's a man
standing nearby on the bank
looking out at the river.

This is not so unusual;
our property adjoins a city park
and public river access.
But I do wonder
what he's doing here at
8:30 in the morning.

My pulse does a quick leap,
like who-the-hell-is-this-maybe-I-should-leave.
I'm rooted to the spot,
a thin five-foot-four sapling.

He's turned away from me —
all I can see is the back of his denim shirt
and same-coloured Levis,
roughed-up cowboy boots
and surprisingly coiffed grey hair.

My foot slips
on some of the twigs.
The man turns around at the sound.
I know that rugged face.

It's Ted Freaking Friesen.

Dialogue

That's what
Ted Friesen
says he wants:
a dialogue about my application.

As though it were perfectly normal
for him to just show up
like this.

(At the same time
I smile inside
remembering that my mom
described him as handsome.
He's *so* her type.)

He says that they
("they" being the Wildwood jury)
were confused by my application.
They couldn't understand why
I burned my first piece.

Goddamned newspaper article.
Otherwise they never would
have known.

They couldn't understand why
I made this new one,
this seemingly last-minute
ephemeral tribute
of sticks and moss.

"They didn't want to accept you,"
he says, and my head goes
woozy at his words.
"But I persuaded them
to let you convince me."

He stands,
facing me,
waiting.

His blue eyes
are patient.
It feels like he'd be willing
to wait the rest of his
life for me to speak.

My eyes wander
over the curves and lines
of the river mermaid.

"I was making meaning,"
I say, finally.

"The beauty queen sculpture
was what I thought the jury would want.

The river mermaid is what
I want."

Ted Friesen nods.

"I met your mother once,"
he says.
"She was a formidable woman.
I'm so sorry."

Then he
squeezes my shoulder,
turns
and goes.

The More I Think About It

Famous artist shows up
at teenage girl's house.
Not even her house —
a rock in her backyard.
They exchange a few words,
then he heads off
like a cowboy riding into the sunset.

The more I think about it
the more surreal
and cinematic
and actually kind of
comical it becomes.

Whatever it was,
whatever happened there

I hope it worked.

Forever

I pull out my phone,
hands quivering.
Text Sandra.

Moments later:

Dude. WTF.

Mercedes of Purple Gables

That's what Ellis calls me
as I lead him through my
bedroom window
out onto the roof.

It's a new moon:
we wanted to make
the most of it.

He knows that Wildwood
is all I'm thinking about
(and his hands
and his cheekbones,
except he doesn't know
that).

We haven't talked about
what it will mean
if I go.

Denial is my forte.

He says,
"I wonder how many more sleeps."

Like a kid
counting down the days
until Christmas.

Waiting

Still nothing.

July: After Eternity

Dear Miss Stowell:

*Thank you for your application to the Wildwood Fine Arts
School. We have reviewed your portfolio and images of your
original piece created for the application.*

I slam the letter down
on the kitchen counter.

Horrible memories from
last year's rejection flood me.

I can't
I can't keep reading.

It sounds like it's
going to be a

No.

Finally, Part 2

We are pleased to offer you acceptance to the Grade 12 Specialty Focus program. We were impressed with your piece, River Mermaid, and the personal story that accompanied it.

Our administrator, Evelyn Varga, will be in touch with you soon regarding registration. Our faculty looks forward to working with you.

Thank you for your interest in our school. We are excited to welcome you to Wildwood!

Sincerely,

Helen Chan
Principal, Wildwood Fine Arts School

On behalf of the Selection Committee

Cheers

I already know where he is.
In his La-Z-Boy,
bowl of salt and vinegar chips
balanced on his belly,
sitcoms blaring.

Without a word,
I stand behind him,
bring the acceptance letter
down in front of his face.

He's in the middle of
shovelling a handful of
Old Dutch into his mouth,
and he pauses,
mid-shovel.

He looks at me,
wide-mouthed and wide-eyed.
I nod.

After a struggle,
getting up out of that
contraption of a chair,
he stands.

It's a dude hug,
quick and back-slapping,
but I'll take it.

Sandra

Woohoo!

**Coming over with
prosecco from my
mom's wine chiller.**

**Come on Stowell,
live a little.
LAOSPT**

I smile at Sandra's text.
I click my
phone to text Ellis.

My thumb hovers.

Then I
slump to the floor,
letter in my lap,
and I think,
shit.

My brain is a jumble.
This is what I wanted.
Right?

The Trouble Is

I don't talk to Ellis until the next day.

We meet at Hot Rocks,
in the indigo of 9:30 p.m.
He and I bum-slide down the rocky path,
brush away branches.

Rising up from the river,
each rock has
enough surface area
to fit us both.

We kiss
as the stars
start to show themselves,
the day's heat warming us,
absorbed in the rock.

It's like we don't
want to talk about
why we're here,
and I don't want to be the one
to start.

"I adore your mind,"
he says after a while.
"And, you know,
other things."

He blushes. Even though
I can't see it,
I know he is.

"I've never met anyone
like you before."

I'm waiting for it.

The "but."

The Trouble Is, Continued

"It'll be long days,"
I say, my voice a whisper.
"And then there's
the homework,
the projects.
I won't have much time
on the weekends."

"Yeah," Ellis says.

Our fingers intertwine,
his thumb curling
around mine.

"We'll be in two
different places,"
I say.

I know we could try,
see how it goes.
Maybe we can scrape
together time on weekends.

But then after Grade 12
there's university,
and new lives, and all of that.

I can't talk. Sobs shudder
through my rib cage.

"I'll miss you," I say.

"I still want to know you,"
he says.
"In some way.
Always."

Now we're both at it,
wiping our noses on our sleeves
and we don't even care.

After a time
we lie back on the rock,
staring up at the stars.
Neither of us
wants to leave.

My first breakup.
This is not how
I imagined it.

It's almost like a
coming together,
before the
divergence.

September 6

6:55 a.m.

This is a stupid hour,
but I'm doing it.

I catch the 701 bus,
waiting at its stop at the mall

to rumble me away
to my future.

Mercedes Stowell, 2003 –

A Canadian found-materials artist based in London, UK.
Known for her use of objects from the natural world,
Stowell has created many critically acclaimed sculptures
and installations that explore themes such as nostalgia and
relationships, including *River Mermaid* (2019), *They Have
Souls* (2025), *Essential* (2030) and the Diamond Award-
winning *Butcher Block* (2033), which recreated her childhood
kitchen using driftwood and stones. Stowell's work has
been exhibited in more than three hundred galleries across
North America, the United Kingdom and Europe. Stowell
holds a BFA magna cum laude from Yale University and an
MFA from Oxford University and has won many awards
all over the world. She is married to prominent architect
Ellis McShay. They have two children.

From *Sculptors of the Modern Era*, 10th edition (2038)

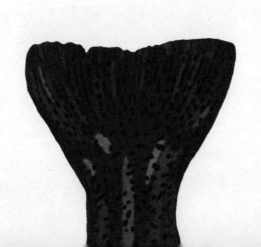

Acknowledgements

I am endlessly grateful for my wonderful creative and
emotional support network — invaluable while writing and
editing novels, and in life in general! A huge thank you to my
magnificent editor and publisher at Crwth Press, Melanie
Jeffs, for her sensitive, brilliant edits and suggestions. My
agent, Barbara Poelle at the Irene Goodman Literary Agency,
took a chance on me with this novel, tirelessly championed
it and helped bring it to fruition — you're the best, B!
Erin Green did both the illustrations and the design of
this gorgeous cover, and perfectly captured the essence
of the novel.

River Mermaid would absolutely not be the book it is today
without the incredible support of my Pitch Wars mentors,
Helene Dunbar and Beth Hull. Thanks to them for seeing a
spark in my draft back then, and allowing me to be part of
such an amazing experience.

My beloved sisters and best friends, Tara and Chay, are
constant sources of support, inspiration, and hilarity, and
I can't imagine life without them. Much gratitude to my
parents — Dan, Cindy, Sher, and my late stepfather Jimbo
— for always supporting my creative projects and endless
daydreams. Keaton and Ione, thank you for putting up with
your often-distracted "writing mode" mother.

Thank you to all who read this book at various stages and offered feedback: Maryn Quarless, Tanya Lloyd Kyi, Kallie George, Rachelle Delaney, Stacey Matson and Lori Sherritt-Fleming. Love and hugs to Amanda Lastoria, Zoë Howard, Colleen Fox, Valerie Miles and Sarah Rosen, who offer inspiration and laughs when I need them the most.

I would like to acknowledge that I wrote this novel on the unceded, unsurrendered lands of the Musqueam, Squamish, and Tsleil-Waututh Nations, as well as the Katzie and Kwantlen Nations. The beautiful landscapes, mountains and rivers of my hometown of Maple Ridge, BC, were a major inspiration for this novel.

Last but definitely not least, a big thank you to the BC Arts Council for their generous funding in support of the novel's early drafts.

About the Author

Born in Maple Ridge, BC, Christy Goerzen has lived most of her adult life in Vancouver, where she works as a university instructor in arts and entertainment management. She has a BA in English and an MA in Children's Literature and is currently working toward her PhD in Education. In her spare time she likes to read, lift heavy things and have random dance parties. Her past novels include *Explore* (2009), *Farmed Out* (2011) and *The Big Apple Effect* (2014), all from Orca Book Publishers. Find her on Twitter and Instagram @glowbuggirl and online at christygoerzenbooks.com.